ABOUT THE TRANSLATORS

Richard Pevear has published translations of Alain, Yves Bonnefoy, Alberto Savinio, Pavel Florensky, and Henri Volohonsky, as well as two books of poetry. He has received fellowships or grants for translation from the National Endowment for the Arts, the Ingram Merrill Foundation, the Guggenheim Foundation, the National Endowment for the Humanities, and the French Ministry of Culture. Larissa Volokhonsky was born in Leningrad. She has translated works by the prominent Orthodox theologians Alexander Schmemann and John Meyendorff into Russian.

Together, Pevear and Volokhonsky have translated *Dead Souls* and *The Collected Tales* by Nikolai Gogol, *The Complete Short Novels* of Chekhov, *Anna Karenina* and *War and Peace* by Leo Tolstoy, and *The Brothers Karamazov, Crime and Punishment, Notes from Underground, Demons, The Idiot, The Adolescent,* and *The Double and The Gambler* by Fyodor Dostoevsky. They were twice awarded the PEN Book-of-the-Month Translation Prize (for their version of Dostoevsky's *The Brothers Karamazov* and for Tolstoy's *Anna Karenina*), and their translation of Dostoevsky's *Demons* was one of three nominees for the same prize. They are married and live in France.

ALSO TRANSLATED BY RICHARD PEVEAR AND LARISSA VOLOKHONSKY

THE BROTHERS KARAMAZOV *by Fyodor Dostoevsky*

CRIME AND PUNISHMENT *by Fyodor Dostoevsky*

NOTES FROM UNDERGROUND *by Fyodor Dostoevsky*

DEMONS *by Fyodor Dostoevsky*

DEAD SOULS *by Nikolai Gogol*

THE ETERNAL HUSBAND AND OTHER STORIES *by Fyodor Dostoevsky*

THE MASTER AND MARGARITA *by Mikhail Bulgakov*

THE COLLECTED TALES OF NIKOLAI GOGOL

ANNA KARENINA *by Leo Tolstoy*

WAR AND PEACE *by Leo Tolstoy*

STORIES *by Anton Chekhov*

THE COMPLETE SHORT NOVELS OF ANTON CHEKHOV

THE IDIOT *by Fyodor Dostoevsky*

THE ADOLESCENT *by Fyodor Dostoevsky*

THE DOUBLE AND THE GAMBLER *by Fyodor Dostoevsky*

THE DEATH OF IVAN ILYICH AND OTHER STORIES *by Leo Tolstoy*

DOCTOR ZHIVAGO *by Boris Pasternak*

The Death of Ivan Ilyich

LEO TOLSTOY

TRANSLATED FROM THE RUSSIAN BY

RICHARD PEVEAR AND LARISSA VOLOKHONSKY

WITH AN INTRODUCTION BY RICHARD PEVEAR

VINTAGE CLASSICS
Vintage Books
A Division of Random House, Inc.
New York

meaning in my life that will not be annihilated by the death that inevitably awaits me?"

The polemical works and pamphlets Tolstoy wrote in the twenty years following that crisis were his attempt to "serve the good" in an external, ideological way, to change the world by his teaching. But the stories he wrote during those same years show how deeply troubled he remained by those questions he tried repeatedly to answer for others. Late in life, he said to Gorky: "If a man has learned to think, no matter what he may think about, he is always thinking of his own death. All philosophers were like that. And what truths can there be, if there is death?" It was this unappeasable anguish, and not the settled positions of his tracts, that nourished Tolstoy's later artistic works, in which the conversions are not rational and collective but mystical, sudden, unique, and the "answers" are almost beyond the reach of words.

The story of Joseph from the book of Genesis came to be Tolstoy's ideal of "good universal art." It is narration reduced to the bare minimum, because, as he wrote in *What Is Art?* (1898), "the feeling contained in this story is so strong that all details except the most necessary . . . are superfluous and would only hinder the conveying of the feeling, and therefore the story is accessible to all people, it touches people of all nations, ranks, ages, has come down to our time, and will live on for thousands of years. But," he adds, "take the details from the best novels of our time and what will remain?" Yet he was unable to achieve that ideal even in the plainest of his later stories. On the contrary, everywhere in them we find the most precisely observed details of time and place, a concentration on the particular, on sights and smells, on the gestures and intonations of characters—on all that was so specific to Tolstoy's genius, to his extraordinary sensual memory and gift of concrete realization. If that were taken away, there would indeed remain a core of universal human experience—Tolstoy was not interested in the topical issues of his time and almost never wrote about them—but there would not be that poetry of reality which had characterized his artistic works from the very beginning.

In *The Good in the Teaching of Tolstoy and Nietzsche*, the philosopher Lev Shestov wrote: "*The Death of Ivan Ilyich*, as an artistic creation, is one of the most precious gems of Tolstoy's work. It is a question mark so black and strong that it shines through the new and radiant colors of that preaching by which Tolstoy wished to make us forget his former doubts." It was the first work Tolstoy published after the crisis described in *A Confession*. Written between 1884 and 1886, *The Death of Ivan Ilyich* shows clearly both a continuity with his earlier work and the artistic changes that resulted from his "conversion." The power of concrete realization is the same, but there is a new brevity, rapidity, and concentration on essentials; an increased formality of construction underscoring the main idea; and a cast of characters not drawn from Tolstoy's own social milieu.

The protagonists of Tolstoy's earlier works are more or less openly autobiographical: Nikolenka Irtenev in the trilogy *Childhood, Boyhood, and Youth*, Olenin in *The Cossacks*, Pierre Bezukhov in *War and Peace*, Levin in *Anna Karenina*. They are self-conscious men, seekers of truth, concerned with their own inner development. The protagonist of *The Death of Ivan Ilyich* is a banal and totally unreflecting man, a state functionary, and, worst of all for Tolstoy, a judge. The germ of the story came from the sudden death, in 1881, at the age of forty-five, of a certain Ivan Ilyich Mechnikov, a prosecutor from the town of Tula, about eight miles from Tolstoy's estate. He had visited Tolstoy once, and in fact Tolstoy had found him an unusual man. In the story, however, he makes him "most ordinary," heaps him with scorn and irony, and then, through a simple but powerful inversion from external to internal, brings him to an extraordinary transformation. The story ends where it began, but with everything changed: "Instead of death there was light."

In *What Is Art?* Tolstoy denounced "the all-confusing concept of beauty" and defined art as "that human activity which consists in one man's consciously conveying to others, by certain external signs, the feelings he has experienced, and in others being infected by those feelings and also experiencing them." The metaphor of infection has a quality of physical closeness, even of violation, about it: infection does not ask for the consent of the infected. But art is also the creation of an image held up for contemplation, and contemplation implies the freedom of the contemplator. The formal qualities of the work create the distance necessary for contemplation. In *The Death of Ivan Ilyich*, the power of infection is certainly there, but the bold, simple, and perfect construction of the story lends it that indispensible distance which makes recognition possible.

RICHARD PEVEAR

The Death of Ivan Ilyich

I

*I*N THE BIG BUILDING of the law courts, during a break in hearing the case of the Melvinskys, the members and the prosecutor met in Ivan Yegorovich Shebek's office, and the conversation turned to the famous Krasovsky case. Fyodor Vassilievich became heated demonstrating non-jurisdiction, Ivan Yegorovich stood his ground; as for Pyotr Ivanovich, not having entered into the argument in the beginning, he took no part in it and was looking through the just-delivered *Gazette*.

"Gentlemen," he said, "Ivan Ilyich is dead!"

"Can it be?"

"Here, read it," he said to Fyodor Vassilievich, handing him the paper still smelling of fresh ink.

Inside a black border was printed: "It is with profound grief that Praskovya Fyodorovna Golovin informs relations and acquaintances of the passing away of her beloved husband, Ivan Ilyich Golovin, member of the Court of Law, which took place on the 4th of February of this year 1882. The funeral will take place on Friday at 1 p.m."

Ivan Ilyich had been a colleague of the assembled gentlemen, and they had all liked him. He had been ill for several weeks; it had been said that his illness was incurable. His post had been kept open for him, but there was an understanding that, in case of his death, Alexeev might be named to his post, and to Alexeev's post either Vinnikov or Shtabel. So that, on hearing of Ivan Ilyich's death, the first thought of each of the gentlemen assembled in the office was of what this death might mean in terms of transfers or promotions of the members themselves or of their acquaintances.

"Now I'll probably get Shtabel's or Vinnikov's post," thought Fyodor Vassilievich. "It was promised to me long ago, and the promotion means a raise of eight hundred roubles, plus office expenses."

"I must now request my brother-in-law's transfer from Kaluga," thought Pyotr Ivanovich. "My wife will be very glad. Now she won't be able to say I've never done anything for her family."

"I thought he would never get on his feet," Pyotr Ivanovich said aloud. "What a pity."

"But what exactly did he have?"

"The doctors couldn't determine. That is, they did, but differently. When I saw him the last time, it seemed to me he'd recover."

"And I haven't visited him since the holidays. I kept meaning to."

"Did he have money?"

"It seems his wife has a little something. But quite insignificant."

"Yes, we'll have to go. They live terribly far away."

"From you, that is. Everything's far from you."

"See, he can't forgive me for living across the river," Pyotr Ivanovich said, smiling at Shebek. And they started talking about the long distances in town and went back to the session.

Apart from the reflections this death called up in each of them about the transfers and possible changes at work that might result from it, the very fact of the death of a close acquaintance called up in all those who heard of it, as always, a feeling of joy that it was he who was dead and not I.

"You see, he's dead, and I'm not," each of them thought or felt. Close acquaintances, Ivan Ilyich's so-called friends, involuntarily thought as well that it would now be necessary for them to fulfill the very boring obligations of decency and go to the funeral service and to the widow on a visit of condolence.

Closest of all were Fyodor Vassilievich and Pyotr Ivanovich.

Pyotr Ivanovich had been Ivan Ilyich's comrade in law school and considered himself as under obligation to him.

Having told his wife over dinner the news of Ivan Ilyich's death and his reflections on the possible transfer of his brother-in-law to their district, Pyotr Ivanovich, without lying down to rest, put on his tailcoat and drove to Ivan Ilyich's.

At the entrance to Ivan Ilyich's apartments stood a carriage and two cabs. Downstairs, in the front hall by the coatrack, leaning against the wall, was a silk-brocaded coffin lid with tassels and freshly polished gold braid. Two ladies in black were taking off their fur coats. One, Ivan Ilyich's sister, he knew; the other was an unknown lady. Pyotr Ivanovich's colleague, Schwartz, was about to come downstairs and, from the topmost step, seeing him enter, stopped and winked at him, as if to say: "Ivan Ilyich made a botch of it; we'll do better, you and I."

Schwartz's face with its English side-whiskers and his whole slim figure in its tailcoat had, as usual, an elegant solemnity, and this solemnity, always in contrast to Schwartz's playful character, had a special piquancy here. So thought Pyotr Ivanovich.

Pyotr Ivanovich let the ladies go ahead of him and slowly followed them up the stairs. Schwartz did not start down, but remained upstairs. Pyotr Ivanovich understood why: he obviously wanted to arrange where to play vint[1] that evening. The ladies went on upstairs to the widow, and Schwartz, with seriously compressed, firm lips and a playful glance, moved his eyebrows to show Pyotr Ivanovich to the right, to the dead man's room.

Pyotr Ivanovich went in, as always happens, with some perplexity about what he was to do there. One thing he did know, that crossing oneself on such occasions never did any harm. Concerning the need to bow at the same time, he was not quite sure, and therefore he chose something in between: going into the room, he began to cross himself and to bow slightly, as it were. At the same time, insofar as his moving hand and head allowed him, he looked around the room. Two young men, one a schoolboy, nephews apparently, were crossing themselves as they left the room. A little old lady stood motionless. And a lady with strangely raised eyebrows was saying something to her in a whisper. A reader in a frock coat, brisk, resolute, was loudly reading something with an expression that precluded all contradiction; the butler's helper, Gerasim, passing in front of Pyotr Ivanovich with light steps, sprinkled something on the floor. Seeing this, Pyotr Ivanovich at once sensed a slight smell of decaying corpse. During his last visit with Ivan Ilyich, Pyotr Ivanovich had seen this muzhik in the study; he had performed the duties of a nurse, and Ivan Ilyich had especially liked him. Pyotr Ivanovich kept crossing himself and bowing slightly in an intermediary direction between the coffin, the reader, and the icons on a table in the corner. Then, when this movement of crossing himself with his hand seemed to have gone on too long, he stopped and began to examine the dead man.

The dead man lay, as dead men always lie, with a peculiar heaviness, dead-man fashion, his stiffened limbs sunk into the lining of the coffin, his forever bent head on the pillow, displaying, as dead men always do, his yellow, waxen forehead with the hair brushed forward on his sunken temples, and his thrust-out nose, as if pressing down on his upper lip. He had changed very much, had grown still thinner, since Pyotr Ivanovich last saw him, but, as with all dead people, his face was more handsome, and above all more significant, than it had been in the living man. There was on his face the expression that what needed to be done had been done, and done rightly. Besides that, there was also in that expression a reproach or a reminder to the living. This reminder seemed out of place to Pyotr Ivanovich, or at least of no concern to him. Something felt unpleasant to him, and therefore Pyotr Ivanovich crossed himself again hastily, too hastily, as it seemed to him, to conform to decency, turned and went to the door. Schwartz was waiting for him in the passage, his legs straddled, his hands playing with his top hat behind his back. One glance at Schwartz's playful, clean, and elegant figure refreshed Pyotr Ivanovich. Pyotr Ivanovich understood that he, Schwartz, was above it all and would not succumb to depressing impressions. His look alone said: the incident of the funeral service for Ivan Ilyich could in no way serve as a sufficient motive for considering the order of the session disrupted, that is, that nothing could prevent them from cracking a newly unsealed deck of cards that same evening, while a valet set up four as yet unlit candles; in general, there were no grounds for supposing that this incident could prevent us from spending that evening pleasantly. He even said so in a whisper to the passing Pyotr Ivanovich, suggesting that they get together for a game at Fyodor Vassilievich's. But Pyotr Ivanovich was evidently not fated to play vint that evening. Praskovya Fyodorovna, a short, fat woman, who, despite all her efforts to achieve the contrary, still broadened from the shoulders down, dressed all in black, her head covered with lace, and with the same strangely raised eyebrows as the lady who had stood facing the coffin, came out of her rooms with other ladies and, accompanying them to the dead man's door, said:

"The service will begin at once; please go in."

Schwartz, bowing indefinitely, stood there, apparently neither accepting nor declining this suggestion. Praskovya Fyodorovna, recognizing Pyotr Ivanovich, sighed, went up close to him, took him by the hand, and said:

"I know you were a true friend of Ivan Ilyich . . ." and looked at him, expecting some action from him that would correspond to those words.

Pyotr Ivanovich knew that, as there he had had to cross himself, so here he had to press her hand, sigh, and say: "Believe me!" And so he did. And, having done that, he felt that the result achieved was the desired one: that he was moved and she was moved.

"Come while it hasn't started yet; I must talk with you," said the widow. "Give me your arm."

Pyotr Ivanovich offered her his arm, and they went to the inner rooms, past Schwartz, who winked mournfully at Pyotr Ivanovich: "There goes our vint! Don't complain if we take another partner. Unless you join us as a fifth when you get free," said his playful glance.

Pyotr Ivanovich sighed still more deeply and mournfully, and Praskovya Fyodorovna gratefully pressed his arm. Having gone into her drawing room, upholstered in pink cretonne and with a sullen lamp, they sat by the table, she on the sofa, Pyotr Ivanovich on a low pouf with bad springs that gave way erratically under his weight. Praskovya Fyodorovna wanted to warn him that he should sit on another chair, but she found such a warning inconsistent with her position and changed her mind. As he sat down on this pouf, Pyotr Ivanovich recalled how Ivan Ilyich had decorated this drawing room and had consulted him about this same cretonne, pink with green leaves. Passing by the table and sitting down on the sofa (generally the whole drawing room was filled with knickknacks and furniture), the widow caught the black lace of her black mantilla on the carving of the table. Pyotr Ivanovich got up to release it, and the pouf, freed from under him, roused itself and gave him a shove. The widow began to release the lace herself, and Pyotr Ivanovich sat down again, crushing the rebellious pouf under him. But the widow did not release it completely, and Pyotr Ivanovich got up again, and again the pouf rebelled and even gave a snap. When all this was over, she took out a clean cambric handkerchief and began to cry. The episode with the lace and the struggle with the pouf cooled Pyotr Ivanovich down, and he sat scowling. This awkward situation was interrupted by Sokolov, Ivan Ilyich's butler, with the report that the plot in the cemetery chosen by Praskovya Fyodorovna would cost two hundred roubles. She stopped crying and, glancing at Pyotr Ivanovich with the air of a victim, said in French that it was very hard for her. Pyotr Ivanovich made a silent gesture expressing the unquestionable conviction that it could not be otherwise.

"Smoke, please," she said in a magnanimous and at the same time brokenhearted voice, and she began to discuss the question of the price of the plot with Sokolov. Pyotr Ivanovich, lighting up, heard her asking in great detail about the prices of various plots and determining which should be taken. Besides that, having finished about the plot, she also gave orders about the choir. Sokolov left.

"I do everything myself," she said to Pyotr Ivanovich, pushing aside the albums that lay on the table; and, noticing that the table was threatened with ashes, she promptly moved an ashtray for Pyotr Ivanovich and said: "I find it false to claim that grief prevents me from concerning myself with practical matters. On the contrary, if anything can, not comfort . . . but distract me, it is my troubles over him." She took out her handkerchief again as if she was about to cry, but suddenly, as if overcoming herself, gave a shake and began to speak calmly:

"However, I have business with you."

Pyotr Ivanovich bowed, not allowing the springs of the pouf, which at once began stirring under him, to act up.

"During the last days he suffered terribly."

"He suffered very much?" asked Pyotr Ivanovich.

"Ah, terribly! The last, not minutes, but hours, he didn't stop screaming. For three days in a row he screamed incessantly. It was unbearable. I can't understand how I endured it. It could be heard through three doors. Ah! what I've endured!"

"And can it be that he was conscious?" asked Pyotr Ivanovich.

"Yes," she whispered, "till the last moment. He said farewell to us a quarter of an hour before he died, and also asked that Volodya be taken away."

The thought of the suffering of a man he had known so closely, first as a merry boy, a schoolmate, then as an adult colleague, despite the unpleasant awareness of his own and this woman's falsity, suddenly terrified Pyotr Ivanovich. He again saw that forehead, the nose pressing on the upper lip, and he felt afraid for himself.

"Three days of terrible suffering and then death. Why, that could come for me, too, right now, any minute," he thought, and he was momentarily afraid. But at once, he did not know how himself, the usual thought came to his aid, that this had happened to Ivan Ilyich and not to him, and that it should and could not happen to him, that in thinking so he had succumbed to a gloomy mood, which ought not to be done, as was obvious from Schwartz's face. And having reasoned thus, Pyotr Ivanovich calmed down and began asking with interest about the details of Ivan Ilyich's end, as if death was an occurrence proper only to Ivan Ilyich, but not at all to him.

After various discussions of the details of the truly terrible physical sufferings endured by Ivan Ilyich (these details Pyotr Ivanovich learned only by the effect of Ivan Ilyich's sufferings on Praskovya Fyodorovna's nerves), the widow evidently found it necessary to proceed to business.

"Ah, Pyotr Ivanovich, it's so hard, so terribly hard, so terribly hard," and she began to cry again.

Pyotr Ivanovich sighed and waited while she blew her nose. When she finished blowing her nose, he said:

"Believe me . . ." and again she fell to talking and told him what was evidently her main business with him; this business consisted in the question of how to obtain money from the treasury on the occasion of her husband's death. She made it seem that she was asking Pyotr Ivanovich's advice about a pension; but he saw that she already knew in the minutest detail things that he did not know, such as all that could be squeezed out of the treasury on the occasion of this death; but that she would like to find out whether it was not possible somehow to squeeze out more. Pyotr Ivanovich tried to think up some way, but, having thought a little and, for decency's sake, having scolded our government for its stinginess, he said it seemed that more was impossible. Then she sighed and obviously began thinking up some way to get rid of her visitor. He understood that, put out his cigarette, got up, pressed her hand, and went to the front hall.

In the dining room with the clock that Ivan Ilyich was so happy to have bought in an antiques shop, Pyotr Ivanovich met a priest and several more acquaintances who had come for the service, and noticed a beautiful young lady of his acquaintance, Ivan Ilyich's daughter. She was all in black. Her waist, which was very slender, seemed more slender still. She had a gloomy, resolute, almost wrathful look. She bowed to Pyotr Ivanovich as if he were to blame for something. Behind the daughter, with the same offended look, stood a rich young man of Pyotr Ivanovich's acquaintance, an examining magistrate, her fiancé as he had heard. He bowed to them dolefully and was about to go into the dead man's room, when from under the stairs appeared the little figure of Ivan Ilyich's schoolboy son, who looked terribly like him. He was a little Ivan Ilyich, as Pyotr Ivanovich remembered him from law school. His eyes were tearful and such as are found in impure boys of thirteen or fourteen. The boy, noticing Pyotr Ivanovich, began to scowl sternly and bashfully. Pyotr Ivanovich nodded to him and went into the dead man's room. The service began—candles, moans, incense, tears, sobs. Pyotr Ivanovich stood frowning, looking at the feet in front of him. He did not glance once at the dead man and throughout did not succumb to weakening influences and was one of the first to leave. There was no one in the front hall. Gerasim, the butler's helper, sprang out of the dead man's room, rummaged with his strong hands through all the fur coats to find Pyotr Ivanovich's coat, and held it for him.

"Well, brother Gerasim?" said Pyotr Ivanovich, just to say something. "A pity, isn't it?"

"It's God's will. We'll all come to it some day," said Gerasim, baring his white, even row of muzhik's teeth, and, like a man in the heat of hard work, briskly opened the door, hailed the coachman, helped Pyotr Ivanovich in, and sprang back to the porch, as if thinking about what else he might do.

Pyotr Ivanovich found it especially pleasant to breathe fresh air after the smell of incense, corpse, and carbolic acid.

"Where to?" asked the coachman.

"It's not late. I can still go to Fyodor Vassilievich's."

And Pyotr Ivanovich went. And indeed he found them at the end of the first rubber, so that it was timely for him to step in as a fifth.

II

THE PAST HISTORY of Ivan Ilyich's life was most simple and ordinary and most terrible.

Ivan Ilyich died at the age of forty-five, a member of the Court of Law. He was the son of an official who had made a career in Petersburg in various ministries and departments, of the sort that brings people to a position in which, though it becomes clear that they are unfit to perform any sort of substantial duties, still, because of their long past service and rank, they cannot be dismissed, and therefore they receive invented, fictitious posts and non-fictitious thousands, from six to ten, on which they live to a ripe old age.

Such was the privy councillor, the unnecessary member of various unnecessary institutions, Ilya Yefimovich Golovin.

He had three sons. Ivan Ilyich was the second son. The eldest had made the same sort of career as his father, only in a different ministry, and was already drawing near that age in the service at which this salaried inertia is attained. The third son was a failure. He had spoiled things for himself in various places and was now serving with the railways; his father and brothers, and especially their wives, not only did not like meeting him, but, unless from the utmost necessity, did not even remember his existence. The sister was married to Baron Greff, the same sort of Petersburg official as his father-in-law. Ivan Ilyich was *le phénix de la famille,** as they said. He was not as cold and meticulous as the elder and not as desperate as the younger. He was between the two—an intelligent, lively, pleasant, and decent man. He was educated together with his younger brother in law school. The younger brother did not finish and was expelled from the fifth class. Ivan Ilyich finished his studies successfully. In law school he was already what he would be throughout his later life: a capable man, cheerfully good-natured and gregarious, but strict in fulfilling what he considered his duty; and he considered his duty all that was so considered by highly placed people. He was not ingratiating, either as a boy or later as an adult, but, from the earliest age he had had this quality of being drawn, as a fly is to light, to the most highly placed people in society, of adopting their manners, their views of life,

---

* The pride of the family.

and of establishing friendly relations with them. All the passions of child-hood and youth went by without leaving big traces on him; he had been given to sensuality and vanity and—towards the end, in the upper classes—to liberalism, but it was all within certain limits, which were correctly pointed out to him by his instinct.

In law school he had committed acts which had formerly seemed to him of great vileness and had inspired a feeling of self-loathing in him at the time he committed them; but subsequently, seeing that such acts were also committed by highly placed people and were not considered bad, he, without really thinking them good, forgot all about them and was not troubled in the least by the memory of them.

On leaving law school in the tenth rank[2] and receiving money from his father to outfit himself, Ivan ordered clothes from Charmeur,[3] hung a little medal on his watch chain inscribed *respice finem,** took his leave of prince and tutor, dined with his schoolmates at Donon's,[4] and with a fashionable new trunk, linen, clothes, shaving and toiletry kits, and a plaid, ordered and purchased at the very best shops, left for the provinces to take a post as official on special missions for the governor, which his father had procured for him.

In the provinces Ivan Ilyich immediately arranged as easy and pleas-ant a situation for himself as his situation in law school had been. He served, made his career, and at the same time amused himself pleasantly and decently; from time to time his superiors sent him on missions to various districts, and he behaved himself with dignity with both those above him and those beneath him, and with precision and incorruptible honesty, which he could not but be proud of, he carried out the missions he was charged with, mostly to do with the Old Believers.[5]

In matters of service, despite his youth and inclination for light merri-ment, he was extremely restrained, official, and even stern; but socially he was often playful and witty, and always good-natured, decent, and *bon enfant,*† as his superior and his wife, with whom he was like one of the family, used to say of him.

There was a liaison in the provinces with one of the ladies who fas-tened upon the foppish lawyer; there was also a milliner; there were

* Look to the end.
† A pleasant fellow.

drinking parties with traveling imperial adjutants, and little trips to a remote back street after supper; there was also subservience to his superior and even to the superior's wife; but it all bore such a lofty tone of propriety that it could not be called by any bad words: it all merely fell under the rubric of the French saying: *Il faut que jeunesse se passe.** It was all done with clean hands, in clean shirts, with French words, and above all in the highest society, consequently with the approval of highly placed people.

So Ivan Ilyich served for five years, and then came changes in the service. New legal institutions appeared; new people were needed.[6]

And Ivan Ilyich became this new man.

Ivan Ilyich was offered a post as examining magistrate, and Ivan Ilyich accepted it, though this post was in another province and he had to abandon the relations he had established and establish new ones. Ivan Ilyich's friends saw him off, had a group photograph taken, offered him a silver cigarette case, and he left for his new post.

As an examining magistrate, Ivan Ilyich was just as *comme il faut*, decent, capable of separating his duties from his private life and of inspiring general respect as he had been as an official on special missions. The work of an examining magistrate was itself far more interesting and attractive for Ivan Ilyich than his previous work. In his previous work, he had found it pleasant to walk at an easy pace, in an undress uniform from Charmeur's, past trembling petitioners waiting to be received and officials envious of him, straight to the superior's office, and sit down with him for tea and a cigarette; but there had been few people directly dependent on his will. Of such people there had been only police officers and Old Believers, when he was sent on special missions; and he had liked to treat such people, who were dependent on him, courteously, almost in a comradely fashion, had liked to let them feel that here was he, who had the power to crush them, treating them in a simple, friendly way. There had been few such people then. Now, though, as an examining magistrate, Ivan Ilyich felt that everyone, everyone without exception, the most important, the most self-satisfied people—everyone was in his hands, and he needed only to write certain words on paper with a letterhead, and this important, self-satisfied man would be brought to

* Youth must have its day.

him as an accused person or a witness, and, if he was not of a mind to let him sit down, the man would stand before him and answer his questions. Ivan Ilyich never misused this power of his; on the contrary, he tried to soften its expression; but for him the consciousness of this power and the possibility of softening it constituted the main interest and attraction of his new work. In that work itself, namely in examinations, Ivan Ilyich very quickly adopted the method of pushing away from himself all circumstances not concerned with service, and investing even the most complicated case in such a form that, on paper, the case was reflected only in its external aspects and his personal views were entirely excluded, and, above all, the required formality was fully observed. This was a new thing. And he was one of the first people to work out the practical application of the statutes of 1864.

Having moved to a new town in the post of examining magistrate, Ivan Ilyich made new acquaintances, connections, behaved in a new way, and adopted a somewhat different tone. He placed himself at a certain dignified remove from the provincial authorities, but chose the best circle of magistrates and rich nobility living in the town, and adopted a tone of slight dissatisfaction with the government, moderate liberalism, and a civilized sense of citizenship. At the same time, without changing his elegant dress in the least, Ivan Ilyich, given his new duties, stopped shaving his chin and gave his beard the freedom to grow where it liked.

Ivan Ilyich's life came together very pleasantly in this new town as well: the society that cast aspersions at the governor was close-knit and agreeable; his salary was higher, and no little pleasure was added to his life by whist, which Ivan Ilyich began to play, having a capacity for playing cards cheerfully, for calculating quickly and subtly, so that generally he always came out the winner.

After two years of service in the new town, Ivan Ilyich met his future wife. Praskovya Fyodorovna Mikhel was the most attractive, intelligent, and brilliant girl of that circle in which Ivan Ilyich moved. Among other amusements and rests from his labors as a magistrate, Ivan Ilyich established light and playful relations with Praskovya Fyodorovna.

Ivan Ilyich, when an official on special missions, had generally danced; now, being an examining magistrate, he danced only as an exception. He now danced in the sense that, while belonging to the new institutions and of the fifth rank,[7] if it comes to dancing, I can demonstrate that in that line I can do better than others. So, from time to time, at the end of an evening, he danced with Praskovya Fyodorovna, and it was mostly during that dancing that he won Praskovya Fyodorovna's heart. She fell in love with him. Ivan Ilyich had no clear, definite intention of marrying, but when the girl fell in love with him, he put the question to himself. "In fact, why not get married?" he said to himself.

Miss Praskovya Fyodorovna was of good noble stock and not bad looking; there was a bit of money. Ivan Ilyich might have counted on a more brilliant match, but this match was also good. Ivan Ilyich had his salary; she, he hoped, would have as much. A good family; she was a sweet, pretty, and perfectly respectable woman. To say that Ivan Ilyich married because he loved his bride and found her sympathetic to his view of life would be as incorrect as to say that he married because people of his society approved of this match. Ivan Ilyich married out of both considerations: he did something pleasant for himself in acquiring such a wife, and at the same time he did what highly placed people considered right.

And so Ivan Ilyich got married.

The process of marriage itself and the initial time of married life, with its conjugal caresses, new furniture, new dishes, new linen, went so well until his wife's pregnancy that Ivan Ilyich was already beginning to think that marriage not only would not disrupt that character of life— easy, pleasant, merry, and always decent and approved of by society— which Ivan Ilyich considered the very essence of life, but would even add to it. But then, with the first months of his wife's pregnancy, there appeared something new, unanticipated, unpleasant, painful, and indecent, which it had been impossible to anticipate and which it was impossible to get rid of.

His wife, without any cause, as it seemed to Ivan Ilyich, *de gaieté de coeur,** as he said to himself, began to disrupt the pleasantness and decency of life: she became jealous over him without any reason, demanded that he court her, found fault with everything, and made unpleasant and crude scenes.

At first Ivan Ilyich hoped to free himself from the unpleasantness of this situation by that same easy and decent attitude towards life which had rescued him before—he tried to ignore his wife's state of mind and went on living as easily and pleasantly as before: invited friends to make

* On a whim.

up a game, tried to get away himself to the club or to see colleagues. But one time his wife began to abuse him so energetically in crude terms, and so stubbornly went on abusing him each time he did not fulfill her demands, obviously firmly resolved not to stop until he submitted, that is, sat at home and was just as bored as she was, that Ivan Ilyich became terrified. He realized that marital life—at least with his wife—was not always conducive to the pleasantness and decency of life, but, on the contrary, often disrupted them, and that it was therefore necessary to protect himself against these disruptions. And Ivan Ilyich began to search for ways of doing that. His work was the one thing that commanded Praskovya Fyodorovna's respect, and Ivan Ilyich, by means of his work and the duties it entailed, began to struggle with his wife, fencing off his independent world.

With the birth of the child, the attempts at nursing and various failures at it, with illnesses, real and imaginary, of the child and the mother, in which it was demanded that he participate, but in which he could understand nothing, Ivan Ilyich's need to fence off a world for himself outside the family became still more imperative.

As his wife became more irritable and demanding, Ivan Ilyich transferred the center of gravity of his life to his work. He came to like his work more and became more ambitious than he had been before.

Very soon, not more than a year after his marriage, Ivan Ilyich understood that marital life, while offering certain conveniences, was essentially a very complex and difficult affair, with regard to which, in order to fulfill one's duty, that is, to lead a decent life approved of by society, one had to work out a certain attitude, as one did to one's work.

And Ivan Ilyich did work out such an attitude to marital life. He demanded of marital life only those comforts of dinner at home, housekeeping, bed, which it could give him, and, above all, that decency of external forms which was defined by public opinion. In the rest he sought a cheerful pleasantness, and if he found it, he was very grateful; if he met with resistance and peevishness, he at once retired to his own separate, fenced-off world of work and found pleasantness in it.

Ivan Ilyich was valued for his good service and three years later was appointed assistant prosecutor. The new duties, their importance, the possibility of calling anyone into court and putting him in jail, the public speeches, the success Ivan Ilyich had in these things—all this attracted him still more to his work.

Children came. His wife was growing more and more peevish and angry, but the attitude to domestic life worked out by Ivan Ilyich made him almost impervious to her peevishness.

After serving for seven years in the same town, Ivan Ilyich was transferred to the post of prosecutor in a different province. They moved, there was too little money, and his wife did not like the place they moved to. The salary was higher than previously, but life was more expensive; besides, two of the children died, and therefore family life became still more unpleasant for Ivan Ilyich.

Praskovya Fyodorovna blamed her husband for all the misfortunes that occurred in this new place of living. Most of the subjects of conversation between husband and wife, especially the children's education, led to problems that were reminiscent of quarrels, and quarrels were ready to flare up at any moment. There remained only rare periods of amorousness that came over the spouses, but they did not last long. These were islands that they would land on temporarily, but then they would put out again to the sea of concealed enmity that expressed itself in estrangement from each other. This estrangement might have upset Ivan Ilyich, if he had considered that it ought not to be so, but by now he took this situation not only as normal, but as the goal of his activity in the family. His goal consisted in freeing himself more and more from these unpleasantnesses and in giving them a character of harmlessness and decency; and he achieved it by spending less and less time with his family, and when he was forced to do so, he tried to secure his position by the presence of outsiders. The main thing was that Ivan Ilyich had his work. The whole interest of life was concentrated for him in the world of his work. And this interest absorbed him. The consciousness of his power, the possibility of destroying any man he wanted to destroy, his importance, even externally, as he entered the court or met with subordinates, his success before his superiors and subordinates, and, above all, his skill in pleading cases, which he was aware of—all this was a cause for joy, and, along with friends, dinners, and whist, filled his life. So that generally the life of Ivan Ilyich continued to go as he thought it should go: pleasantly and decently.

He lived that way for another seven years. The eldest daughter was already sixteen, one more child had died, and there remained the young schoolboy, a subject of contention. Ivan Ilyich wanted to send him to law school, but Praskovya Fyodorovna, to spite him, sent him to preparatory school. The daughter studied at home and was growing up nicely; the boy was also not a bad student.

III

SO WENT Ivan Ilyich's life during the seventeen years following his marriage. He was already a seasoned prosecutor, who had turned down several transfers in expectation of a more desirable post, when a certain unpleasant circumstance unexpectedly occurred, which all but disrupted the tranquillity of his life. Ivan Ilyich was expecting the post of presiding judge in a university town, but Hoppe somehow beat him out and got the post. Ivan Ilyich became irritated, reproached him, and quarreled with him and his immediate superior; he was treated with coldness and at the next promotions he was again passed over.

That was in the year 1880. That year was the hardest of Ivan Ilyich's life. In that year it turned out, on the one hand, that his salary was not enough to live on; and on the other, that everyone had forgotten him, and that what seemed to him the greatest, cruelest injustice in his regard, others saw as a perfectly ordinary matter. Even his father did not consider it his duty to help him. He felt that everyone had abandoned him, considering his position with its 3,500-rouble salary as most normal and even fortunate. He alone knew that, with the consciousness of the injustice done him, with his wife's eternal carping, and with the debts he began to run up, living beyond his means—he alone knew that his position was far from normal.

In the summer of that year, to lighten his expenses, he took a vacation and went with his wife to spend the summer in the country with Praskovya Fyodorovna's brother.

In the country, without work, Ivan Ilyich felt for the first time not merely boredom, but an unbearable anguish, and he decided that it was impossible to live like that, and that it was necessary to take decisive measures.

Having spent a sleepless night, pacing the terrace the whole time, Ivan Ilyich decided to go to Petersburg to solicit for himself, and, so as to punish *them* for not knowing how to appreciate him, to transfer to another ministry.

The next day, despite all the attempts of his wife and brother-in-law to dissuade him, he went to Petersburg.

He went with one purpose: to solicit a post with a salary of five thousand. He no longer adhered to any ministry, tendency, or kind of activity. He only needed a post, a post with five thousand, in the administration, in a bank, in the railways, in the empress Maria's institutions,[8] even in customs, but he had to have five thousand and to leave the ministry where they had not known how to appreciate him.

And, lo and behold, this trip of Ivan Ilyich's was crowned with astonishing, unexpected success. In Kursk an acquaintance, F. S. Ilyin, seated himself in first class and told him about a fresh telegram received by the governor of Kursk saying that there was to be an upheaval in the ministry in a few days: Ivan Semyonovich was appointed to replace Pyotr Ivanovich.

The proposed upheaval, besides its significance for Russia, had a special significance for Ivan Ilyich in that, by bringing forward a new person, Pyotr Petrovich, and, obviously, his friend Zakhar Ivanovich, it was highly favorable for Ivan Ilyich. Zakhar Ivanovich was a colleague and friend of Ivan Ilyich.

In Moscow the news was confirmed. On arriving in Petersburg, Ivan Ilyich found Zakhar Ivanovich and received the firm promise of a post in his former Ministry of Justice.

A week later he sent a telegram to his wife: "Zakhar to replace Miller I get appointment in first memorandum."

Owing to this change of personnel, Ivan Ilyich unexpectedly received an appointment in his former ministry that placed him two steps higher than his old colleagues, with a salary of five thousand, and three thousand five hundred for moving expenses. All his vexation with his former enemies and the entire ministry was forgotten, and Ivan Ilyich was completely happy.

Ivan Ilyich returned to the country cheerful, content, as he had not been for a long time. Praskovya Fyodorovna also cheered up, and a truce was concluded between them. Ivan Ilyich told her how he had been fêted in Petersburg, how all those who had been his enemies were put to shame and now fawned on him, how they envied his post, and, particularly, how loved he was in Petersburg.

Praskovya Fyodorovna listened to all this and pretended to believe it, and did not contradict him in anything, but only made plans for a new arrangement of life in the town they were moving to. And Ivan Ilyich was glad to see that those plans were his plans, that they agreed, and that his faltering life was again acquiring its true, natural character of cheerful pleasantness and decency.

Ivan Ilyich came for only a short time. On September 10th he had to take up his post, and, besides, he needed time to settle into a new place, to transport everything from the province, to buy, to order still more; in short, to arrange things as it had been decided in his mind, and almost exactly as it had been decided in Praskovya Fyodorovna's heart.

And now that everything had arranged itself so fortunately, and he and his wife agreed in their aims, and, besides that, lived together so little, they became such friends as they had not been since the first years of their married life. Ivan Ilyich had first thought of taking his family away at once, but his sister-in-law and her husband suddenly became so especially amiable and familial towards Ivan Ilyich and his family that, at their insistence, Ivan Ilyich left alone.

Ivan Ilyich left, and the cheerful state of mind produced by his success and his agreement with his wife, the one intensifying the other, stayed with him all the while. A charming apartment was found, exactly what the husband and wife were dreaming of. Vast, high-ceilinged reception rooms in the old style, a comfortable and grandiose study, rooms for his wife and daughter, a schoolroom for his son—everything as if purposely designed for them. Ivan Ilyich himself took up the decoration, chose the wallpaper, bought furniture, especially antiques, which he had upholstered in an especially *comme il faut* style, and it all grew, grew and approached that ideal which he had formed for himself. When it was half done, the result exceeded his expectations. He perceived what a *comme il faut*, exquisite, and by no means banal character it would all take on when it was finished. Falling asleep, he imagined how the reception room was going to be. Looking at the as yet unfinished drawing room, he already saw the fireplace, the screen, the whatnot, and those little chairs scattered around, those dishes and plates on the walls, and the bronzes, when they were all put in place. He rejoiced at the thought of how he would astonish Pasha and Lizanka, who also had a taste for these things. They would never expect it. In particular, he managed to find and buy cheaply antique objects that endowed everything with a particularly noble character. In his letters he deliberately presented everything as worse than it was, in order to astonish them. All this occupied him so much that even his new duties, fond as he was of the work, occupied him less than he had expected. During sessions he had moments of distraction: he was pondering what sort of cornices to have for the curtains, straight or festooned. He was so taken up with it that he often pottered about himself, even moved furniture and rehung curtains himself. Once he climbed a ladder to show the uncomprehending upholsterer how he wanted the drapery done, missed his footing, and fell, but, being a strong and agile man, held on and only bumped his side on the knob of the window frame. The bruised place ached for a while, but soon stopped. All this time Ivan Ilyich felt especially cheerful and healthy. He wrote: "I feel as if I've shaken off fifteen years." He hoped to finish in September, but it took until the middle of October. The result was charming—as not only he said, but all those who saw it said to him.

Essentially, though, it was the same as with all people who are not exactly rich, but who want to resemble the rich, and for that reason only resemble each other: damasks, ebony, flowers, carpets, and bronzes, dark and gleaming—all that all people of a certain kind acquire in order to resemble all people of a certain kind. And in his case the resemblance was such that it was even impossible for it to attract attention; but to him it all seemed something special. When he met his family at the railway station, brought them to his brightly lit, finished apartment, and a footman in a white tie opened the door to the flower-decked front hall, and they then went on to the drawing room, the study, and gasped with pleasure— he was very happy, showed them all around, drank in their praises, and beamed with pleasure. That same evening, over tea, when Praskovya Fyodorovna asked him, among other things, how he had fallen, he laughed and acted out how he had gone flying and frightened the upholsterer.

"It's not for nothing I'm a gymnast. Another man might have been badly hurt, but I just got a slight knock here; it hurts when you touch it, but it's already going away; a simple bruise."

And they began to live in their new lodgings, in which, as always, once they had settled nicely, there was just one room lacking, and on their new means, which, as always, were lacking just a little—some five hundred roubles—and it was very nice. Especially nice was the initial time, when all was not arranged yet and still needed arranging: this to buy, that to order, this to move, that to adjust. Though there were some disagreements between husband and wife, they were both so content and there was so much to do that it all ended without any big quarrels. When there was nothing more to arrange, it became slightly boring and lacking in something, but by then they were making acquaintances, habits, and life became full.

Ivan Ilyich, having spent the morning in court, would come home for dinner, and in the initial time his state of mind was good, though it did suffer slightly on account of the lodgings. (Each spot on the tablecloth, on the damask, a torn-out curtain pull, annoyed him: he had put so much labor into arranging it that any damage was painful to him.) But in general Ivan Ilyich's life went on as he believed life ought to go: easily, pleasantly, and decently. He got up at nine, had coffee, read the newspaper, then put on his uniform and went to court. There the yoke in which he worked was already broken in; he fell into it at once. The petitioners, the inquiries in the chancery, the chancery itself, the court sessions—public and administrative. In all this one had to know how to exclude all that was raw, vital—which always disrupts the regular flow of official business; one had to allow no relations with people apart from official ones, and the cause of the relations must be only official and the relations themselves only official. For instance, a man comes and wishes to find something out. As an unofficial man Ivan Ilyich can have no relations with such a man; but if there are relations with this man as a colleague, such as can be expressed on paper with a letterhead, then within the limits of those relations Ivan Ilyich does everything, decidedly everything he can, and with that observes a semblance of friendly human relations, that is, of politeness. As soon as the official relations are ended, all others are ended as well. This skill in separating the official side, not mixing it with his real life, Ivan Ilyich had mastered in the highest degree and through long practice and talent had developed to such a degree that, like a virtuoso, he sometimes allowed himself, as if jokingly, to mix human and official relations. He allowed himself that because he felt himself always capable of separating the official when he needed to and of discarding the human. For Ivan Ilyich this business went not only easily, pleasantly, and decently, but even with virtuosity. During recesses he smoked, drank tea, conversed a little about politics, a little about general matters, a little about cards, and most of all about promotions. And, weary, but with the feeling of a virtuoso who has given a perfect performance of his part as one of the first violins in the orchestra, he returned home. At home, the daughter and mother had been out somewhere or had someone else with them; the son had been to school, had prepared his lessons with his tutors, and was diligently studying what they teach in school. All was well. After dinner, if there were no visitors, Ivan Ilyich sometimes read a book which was being much talked about, and in the evening he sat down to work, that is, read papers, consulted the laws—compared testimony and applied the laws to it. For him this was neither boring nor amusing. It was boring when there might have been a game of vint; but if there was no vint, it was still better than sitting alone or with his wife. But Ivan Ilyich's real pleasure was in little dinners, to which he invited ladies and gentlemen of important social position and passed the time with them similarly to the way such people usually pass the time, just as his drawing room was similar to all other drawing rooms.

Once they even had a soirée with dancing. And Ivan Ilyich was merry, and everything was nice, only a big quarrel broke out with his wife over the cakes and sweets. Praskovya Fyodorovna had her own plan, but Ivan Ilyich insisted on buying everything from an expensive pastry shop, and he bought a lot of cakes, and the quarrel was about the fact that there were cakes left over and the bill from the pastry shop was for forty-five roubles. The quarrel was big and unpleasant, and Praskovya Fyodorovna called him "fool" and "slouch." And he clutched his head and angrily said something about divorce. But the soirée itself was merry. The best society was there, and Ivan Ilyich danced with Princess Trufonov, the sister of the one famous for founding the society "Quench Thou My Grief." The official joys were the joys of self-esteem; the social joys were the joys of vainglory; but Ivan Ilyich's real joys were the joys of playing vint. He admitted that after anything, after whatever joyless events there might be in his life, the joy which, like a candle, burned before all others—was to sit down to vint with good players and soft-spoken partners, a foursome without fail (with a fivesome it was very painful to sit out, though one always pretended to like it), and to carry on an intelligent, serious game (when the cards came your way), then have supper and drink a glass of wine. And Ivan Ilyich went to bed in an especially good humor after vint, especially when he had won a little (to win a lot was unpleasant).

So they lived. The social circle that formed around them was of the best sort; they were visited by important people and by young people.

In their view of the circle of their acquaintances, husband, wife, and daughter agreed completely and, without prearrangement, in the same way fended off and freed themselves from various friends and relations, ragtag people, who came flying with tender feelings to their drawing room with the Japanese dishes on the walls. Soon these ragtag friends stopped flying, and the Golovins remained surrounded by only the best society. Young men courted Lizanka, and Petrishchev, the son of Dmitri Ivanovich Petrishchev and sole heir to his fortune, an examining magistrate, began courting Liza, so that Ivan Ilyich even mentioned it to Praskovya Fyodorovna: perhaps they should arrange a ride together in a troika, or organize theatricals. So they lived. And it all went on like this without change, and it was all very well.

IV

THEY WERE all in good health. It could not be called ill health that Ivan Ilyich sometimes said he had a strange taste in his mouth and some discomfort on the left side of his stomach.

But it so happened that this discomfort began to increase and turn, not into pain yet, but into the consciousness of a constant heaviness in his side and into ill humor. This ill humor, growing stronger and stronger, began to spoil the pleasantness of the easy and decent life that had just been established in the Golovin family. The husband and wife began to quarrel more and more often, and soon the ease and pleasantness fell away, and decency alone was maintained with difficulty. Scenes again became frequent. Again only little islands were left, and few of them, where the husband and wife could come together without an explosion.

And now Praskovya Fyodorovna could say, not without grounds, that her husband had a difficult character. With the habit of exaggeration typical of her, she said that he had always had a terrible character, and it had needed all her goodness to put up with it for twenty years. It was true that the quarrels now began with him. His carping always began just before dinner and often precisely as he was beginning to eat, over the soup. He would point out that something was wrong with one of the plates, or that the food was not right, or that his son had his elbow on the table, or it was his daughter's hairstyle. And he blamed Praskovya Fyodorovna for it all. At first Praskovya Fyodorovna protested and said unpleasant things to him, but twice at the start of dinner he flew into such a rage that she realized it was a morbid condition provoked in him by the taking of food, and she restrained herself; she no longer protested, but only hurried with dinner. Her restraint Praskovya Fyodorovna set down to her own great credit. Having decided that her husband had a terrible character and made her life miserable, she began to pity herself. And the more she pitied herself, the more she hated her husband. She began to wish for his death, yet she could not wish for it, because then there would be no salary. And that irritated her against him still more. She considered herself dreadfully wretched precisely in that even his death could not save her, and she became irritated, concealed it, and this concealed irritation of hers increased his irritation.

After one scene in which Ivan Ilyich was particularly unfair and after which, talking it over with her, he said that he was in fact irritable, but that it was from illness, she told him that, if he was ill, he ought to be treated, and demanded that he go to a famous doctor.

He went. It was all as he expected; it was all as it is always done. The waiting, and the assumed doctorly importance familiar to him, the same that he knew in himself in court, and the tapping, and the auscultation, and the questions calling for predetermined and obviously unnecessary answers, and the significant air, which suggested that you just submit to us, and we will arrange it all—we know indubitably how to arrange it all, all in the same way as for anybody you like. It was all exactly the same as in court. As he put on airs before the accused in court, so the famous doctor put on airs before him.

The doctor said: Such-and-such indicates that there is such-and-such inside you; but if that is not confirmed by the analysis of this-and-that, then it must be assumed that you have such-and-such. If we presume such-and-such, then . . . and so on. For Ivan Ilyich only one question mattered: was his condition dangerous or not? But the doctor ignored this inappropriate question. From the doctor's point of view it was an idle question and not to be discussed; there existed only the weighing of probabilities—a floating kidney, chronic catarrh, or appendicitis. It was not a question of Ivan Ilyich's life, but an argument between a floating kidney and the appendix. And before Ivan Ilyich's very eyes the doctor resolved this argument most brilliantly in favor of the appendix, with the reservation that the urine analysis might give new evidence and the case would then be reconsidered. All this was just exactly what Ivan Ilyich himself had performed as brilliantly a thousand times over the accused. The doctor performed his summing up just as brilliantly, and triumphantly, even merrily, glanced over his spectacles at the accused. From the doctor's summing up, Ivan Ilyich drew the conclusion that things were bad, and that for him, the doctor, and for anyone else you like, it was all the same, but for him things were bad. And this conclusion struck Ivan Ilyich painfully, calling up in him a feeling of great pity for himself and great anger at this doctor, who was indifferent to such an important question.

But he said nothing, got up, put money on the table, and sighed.

"We sick people probably often ask you inappropriate questions," he said. "But, generally, is it a dangerous illness or not? . . ."

The doctor glanced at him sternly with one eye through his spectacles, as if to say: Accused, if you do not keep within the limits of the questions put to you, I will be forced to order you removed from the court.

"I've already told you what I consider necessary and appropriate," said the doctor. "The analysis will give further evidence." And the doctor bowed.

Ivan Ilyich went out slowly, climbed dejectedly into the sleigh, and drove home. On the way he kept going over what the doctor had said, trying to translate all those complicated, vague scientific terms into simple language and read in them the answer to the question: bad—is it very bad for me, or still all right? And it seemed to him that the sense of everything the doctor had said was that it was very bad. Everything seemed sad to Ivan Ilyich in the streets. The cabbies were sad, the houses were sad, the passersby and the shops were sad. And that pain, the obscure, gnawing pain, which did not cease for a moment, seemed to have acquired, in connection with the doctor's vague words, a different, more serious meaning. With a new, heavy feeling Ivan Ilyich now paid heed to it.

He came home and started telling his wife. His wife listened, but in the middle of his account his daughter came in with her hat on: she and her mother were going somewhere. She forced herself to sit down and listen to this boredom, but could not stand it for long, and the mother did not hear him out.

"Well, I'm very glad," said his wife, "so now see to it that you take your medicine regularly. Give me the prescription, I'll send Gerasim to the pharmacy." And she went to get dressed.

He could not breathe freely while she was in the room and sighed heavily when she left.

"Oh, well," he said. "Maybe in fact it's all right . . ."

He began to take medicines, following the doctor's prescriptions, which were changed on account of the urine analysis. But then it just so happened that, in this analysis and in what should have followed from it, there was some sort of confusion. It was impossible to reach the doctor himself, and meanwhile what was being done was not what the doctor had said to him. He either forgot, or lied, or was hiding something from him.

But all the same Ivan Ilyich started following the prescriptions precisely and in following them found comfort at first.

Ivan Ilyich's main occupation since the time of his visit to the doctor became the precise following of the doctor's prescriptions concerning hygiene and the taking of medicines, and paying heed to his pain and to all the functions of his organism. People's illness and people's health became Ivan Ilyich's main interests. When there was talk in his presence of someone being ill, or dying, or recovering, especially of an illness similar to his own, he listened, trying to conceal his excitement, asked questions, and made applications to his illness.

The pain did not diminish; but Ivan Ilyich tried to make himself think that he was better. And he could deceive himself as long as nothing worried him. But as soon as there was some unpleasantness with his wife, a setback at work, or bad cards at vint, he immediately felt the whole force of his illness; he used to endure these setbacks, expecting to quickly right the wrong, to overcome it, to achieve success, a grand slam. But now any setback undercut him and threw him into despair. He said to himself: I was just getting better, and the medicine was beginning to work, and here's this cursed misfortune or unpleasantness . . . And he became angry at the misfortune or at the people who had caused him the unpleasantness and were killing him; and he felt how this anger was killing him, but he could not repress it. It seems it ought to have been clear to him that this anger at circumstances and at people was aggravating his illness, and that therefore he should not pay attention to unpleasant occasions; but his reasoning was quite the opposite: he said that he needed peace, looked out for anything that might disturb that peace, and at the slightest disturbance became irritated. His condition was also made worse by his reading of medical books and consulting of doctors. The worsening went on so gradually that he could deceive himself comparing one day with another—the difference was so slight. But when he consulted doctors, it seemed to him that it was getting worse and even very quickly. And despite that, he constantly consulted doctors.

That month he visited yet another celebrity: the other celebrity said almost the same thing as the first, but put his questions differently. And the consultation with this celebrity only increased Ivan Ilyich's doubt and fear. The friend of a friend of his—a very good doctor—defined the illness in quite another way still and, though he promised recovery, his questions and conjectures confused Ivan Ilyich still more and increased his doubts. A homeopath defined the illness in still another way and gave him medicine, and Ivan Ilyich, in secret from everyone, took it for a week. But after a week, feeling no relief and losing confidence both in the former treatments and in this one, he fell into still greater dejection. Once a lady acquaintance told about healing with icons. Ivan Ilyich caught himself listening attentively and believing in the reality of the fact. This occasion frightened him. "Can I have grown so mentally feeble?" he said to himself. "Nonsense! It's all rubbish, I mustn't give way to anxieties, but choose one doctor and keep strictly to his treatment. That's what I'll do. It's over now. I won't think, and I'll strictly follow the treatment till summer. Then we'll see. These vacillations are over now! . . ." That was easy to say, but impossible to do. The pain in his side kept gnawing at him, seemed to be increasing, becoming constant; the taste in his mouth kept becoming stranger; it seemed to him that his mouth gave off a disgusting smell, and his appetite and strength kept weakening. It was impossible to deceive himself: something dreadful, new, and so significant that nothing more significant had ever happened in his life, was being accomplished in Ivan Ilyich. And he alone knew of it. Everyone around him either did not understand or did not want to understand and thought that everything in the world was going on as before. This was what tormented Ivan Ilyich most of all. He saw that his household—mainly his wife and daughter, who were in the very heat of social life—did not understand anything, were vexed that he was so cheerless and demanding, as if he was to blame for it. Though they tried to conceal it, he saw that he was a hindrance to them, but that his wife had worked out for herself a certain attitude towards his illness and held to it regardless of what he said and did. This attitude was the following:

"You know," she would say to acquaintances, "Ivan Ilyich cannot keep strictly to the treatment he's prescribed, as all good people do. Today he takes his drops and eats what he's been told to and goes to bed on time; tomorrow suddenly, if I don't look out, he forgets to take them, eats sturgeon (which is forbidden), and stays up till one o'clock playing vint."

"Well, when was that?" Ivan Ilyich would ask with vexation. "Once at Pyotr Ivanovich's."

"And last night with Shebek."

"Anyway I couldn't sleep from pain."

"Whatever the reasons, you'll never get well like this, and you're tormenting us."

Praskovya Fyodorovna's external attitude to her husband's illness, which she voiced to others and to him, was that Ivan Ilyich himself was to blame for the illness and that this whole illness was a new unpleasantness he was causing his wife. Ivan Ilyich felt that this came from her involuntarily, but that did not make it easier for him.

In court Ivan Ilyich noticed or thought he noticed the same strange attitude towards himself: now it seemed to him that he was being eyed like someone who would soon have to vacate his post; now his colleagues suddenly began to joke in friendly fashion about his anxieties, as if that terrible and dreadful unheard-of thing that was sitting in him and ceaselessly gnawing at him and inexorably drawing him somewhere was a most pleasant subject for jokes. Schwartz especially irritated him with his playfulness, vitality, and *comme il faut*-ishness, which reminded Ivan Ilyich of himself ten years ago.

Friends would come for a game, sit down. They dealt, flexing the new cards, sorting diamonds with diamonds, seven of them. His partner bid no trump and opened with two diamonds. What more could one wish for? It should all go cheerfully, briskly—a grand slam. And suddenly Ivan Ilyich feels that gnawing pain, that taste in his mouth, and it seems wild to him that at the same time he should rejoice at a grand slam.

He looks at Mikhail Mikhailovich, his partner, striking the table with a sanguine hand and refraining, politely and indulgently, from picking up the tricks, but moving them towards Ivan Ilyich, so as to give him the pleasure of collecting them without taking the trouble to reach out his hand. "Does he think I'm so weak that I can't reach that far?" Ivan Ilyich thinks, forgets about the trumps and double trumps his own, and loses the slam by three tricks, and most terrible of all is that he sees how Mikhail Mikhailovich suffers and it makes no difference to him. And it is terrible to think why it makes no difference to him.

Everyone sees that it is hard for him, and they say: "We can quit if you're tired. Get some rest." Rest? No, he is not the least bit tired, and they play out the rubber. Everyone is gloomy and silent. Ivan Ilyich feels that it is he who has cast this gloom over them, and he cannot disperse it. They eat supper and go home, and Ivan Ilyich is left alone with the consciousness that his life is poisoned for him and poisons life for others, and that this poison is not weakening but is permeating his whole being more and more.

And with this consciousness, along with physical pain, along with terror, he had to go to bed and often not sleep from pain for the better part of the night. And the next morning he had to get up, dress, go to court, talk, write, and if he did not go, stay at home with the same twenty-four hours in a day, every one of which was torture. And he had to live alone on the brink of disaster like that, without a single human being who could understand and pity him.

V

SO A MONTH went by, then two. Before the New Year his brother-in-law came to their town and stayed with them. Ivan Ilyich was in court. Praskovya Fyodorovna had gone shopping. Going into his study, he found his brother-in-law there, a healthy, sanguine fellow, unpacking his suitcase. On hearing Ivan Ilyich's footsteps, he raised his head and looked at him silently for a moment. That look revealed everything to Ivan Ilyich. The brother-in-law opened his mouth to gasp, but checked himself. This movement confirmed everything.

"What, have I changed?"

"Yes . . . there's a change."

And much as he tried after that to bring his brother-in-law around to talking about his external appearance, the brother-in-law would say nothing. Praskovya Fyodorovna came home, and the brother-in-law went to her. Ivan Ilyich locked the door and started looking in the mirror—full face, then profile. He picked up his portrait with his wife and compared it with what he saw in the mirror. The change was enormous. Then he bared his arms to the elbow, looked, pulled his sleeves down, sat on the ottoman, and turned darker than night.

"Don't, don't," he said to himself, jumped to his feet, went to the desk, opened a brief, started reading it, but could not. He unlocked the door, went to the reception room. The door to the drawing room was shut. He went up to it on tiptoe and started listening.

"No, you're exaggerating," Praskovya Fyodorovna was saying.

"How 'exaggerating'? Don't you see—he's a dead man, look in his eyes. No light. What's wrong with him?"

"Nobody knows. Nikolaev" (this was another doctor) "said something, but I don't know. Leshchetitsky" (this was the famous doctor) "said on the contrary . . ."

Ivan Ilyich stepped away, went to his room, lay down, and began to think: "A kidney, a floating kidney." He remembered all that the doctors had told him, how it had detached itself, and how it floats. By an effort of imagination he tried to catch this kidney and stop it, fasten it down; so little was needed, it seemed to him. "No, I'll go to see Pyotr Ivanovich again." (This was the friend who had the doctor friend.) He rang the bell, ordered the horse harnessed, and made ready to go.

"Where are you off to, Jean?" his wife asked with an especially sad and unusually kind expression.

This unusual kindness angered him. He gave her a dark look.

"I must go to see Pyotr Ivanovich."

He went to see his friend who had the doctor friend. And with him to the doctor. He found him in and had a long conversation with him.

On examining the anatomical and physiological details of what, in the doctor's opinion, was going on inside him, he understood everything.

There was a little thing, a tiny little thing, in the appendix. This could all be put right. Strengthen the energy of one organ, weaken the functioning of another, absorption would take place, and all would be put right. He was a little late for dinner. He dined, talked cheerfully, but for a long while could not go and get busy. Finally he went to his study and at once sat down to work. He read briefs, worked, but the awareness that he had put off an important, intimate matter, which he would take up once he had finished, never left him. When he finished work, he remembered that this intimate matter was the thought of his appendix. But he did not give in to it, he went to the drawing room for tea. There were guests; they talked, played the piano, sang; there was the examining magistrate, their daughter's desired fiancé. Ivan Ilyich spent the evening, as Praskovya Fyodorovna remarked, more cheerfully than others, but never for a moment did he forget that he had put off the important thought of his appendix. At eleven o'clock he said good-night and went to his room. He had slept alone since the time of his illness, in a small room by his study. He went there, undressed, took a novel by Zola but did not read it, and thought. In his imagination the desired mending of the appendix was taking place. Absorption, ejection, restoration of the correct functioning. "Yes, that's all so," he said to himself. "One need only assist nature." He remembered about his medicine, got up, took it, and lay on his back, waiting to feel the beneficial effect of the medicine and how it killed the pain. "Just take it regularly and avoid harmful influences; even now I feel a little better, a lot better." He began to touch his side—it did not hurt. "Yes, I don't feel it, truly, it's already much better." He put out the candle and lay on his side . . . The appendix was mending, absorbing. Suddenly he felt the old familiar, dull, gnawing pain, stubborn, quiet, serious. In his mouth the same familiar vileness. His heart shrank, his head clouded. "My God, my God!" he said. "Again, again, and it will never stop." And suddenly he pictured the matter from an entirely different side. "The appendix! The kidney!" he said to himself. "This is not a matter of the appendix or the kidney, but of life and . . . death. Yes, there was life, and now it is going, going, and I cannot hold it back. Yes, why deceive myself? Isn't it obvious to everybody except me that I'm dying and it is only a question of the number of weeks, days—right now, maybe. Once there was light, now there's darkness. Once I was here, and now I'll be there! Where?" Cold came over him, his breath stopped. He heard only the pounding of his heart.

"There will be no me, so what will there be? There will be nothing. So where will I be, when there's no me? Can this be death? No, I don't want it." He jumped up, wanted to light a candle, felt around with trembling hands, dropped the candle and candlestick on the floor, and fell back on the pillow again. "What for? It makes no difference," he said to himself, gazing wide-eyed into the darkness. "Death. Yes, death. And none of them knows, or wants to know, or feels pity. They're playing." (He heard through the door the distant roll of a voice and ritornello.) "It makes no difference to them, but they'll also die. Fools. For me sooner, for them later; but it will be the same for them. Yet they make merry. Brutes!" He was choking with anger. And he felt tormentingly, unbearably oppressed. It just can't be that everyone has always been condemned to this terrible fear. He sat up.

"Something's not right. I must calm down; I must think it over from the beginning." And so he began to think it over. "Yes, the beginning of the illness. I bumped my side, and then I was just the same, that day and the next; it ached a little, then more, then doctors, then dejection, anguish, doctors again; and I was coming closer and closer to the abyss. Losing strength. Closer and closer. And here I am wasted away, there's no light in my eyes. It's death, yet I think about my appendix. I think about repairing my appendix, yet it's death. Can it be death?" Again terror came over him, he gasped for breath, bent down, began searching for the matches, leaned his elbow on the night table. It hindered him and hurt him, he became angry with it, vexedly leaned still harder, and the night table fell over. In despair, suffocating, he fell on his back, expecting death at once.

The guests were just leaving. Praskovya Fyodorovna was seeing them off. She heard something fall and came in.

"What's the matter?"

"Nothing. I tipped it over by accident."

She went out and came back with a candle. He was lying there, breathing heavily and very rapidly, like a man who has run a mile, looking at her with a fixed gaze.

"What's the matter, Jean?"

"Nothing. I tipped it over." ("No use talking. She won't understand," he thought.)

In fact she did not understand. She picked up the night table, lit the candle, and left hastily: she had to see off a lady guest.

When she returned, he was lying on his back in the same way, looking up.

"What is it, are you worse?"

"Yes."

She shook her head and sat down.

"You know, Jean, I think we ought to invite Leshchetitsky to the house."

This meant inviting the famous doctor and not minding the cost. He smiled venomously and said: "No." She sat for a while, went over, and kissed him on the forehead.

He hated her with all the forces of his soul while she was kissing him, and had a hard time not pushing her away.

"Good night. God grant you fall asleep."

"Yes."

VI

IVAN ILYICH SAW that he was dying, and he was in continual despair.

In the depths of his soul Ivan Ilyich knew that he was dying, but not only was he not accustomed to it, he simply did not, he could not possibly understand it.

The example of a syllogism he had studied in Kiesewetter's logic[9]— Caius is a man, men are mortal, therefore Caius is mortal—had seemed to him all his life to be correct only in relation to Caius, but by no means to himself. For the man Caius, man in general, it was perfectly correct; but he was not Caius and not man in general, he had always been quite, quite separate from all other beings; he was Vanya, with mamá, with papá, with Mitya and Volodya, with toys, the coachman, with a nanny, then with Katenka, with all the joys, griefs, and delights of childhood, boyhood, youth. Was it for Caius, the smell of the striped leather ball that Vanya had loved so much? Was it Caius who had kissed his mother's hand like that, and was it for Caius that the silk folds of his mother's dress had rustled like that? Was it he who had mutinied against bad food in law school? Was it Caius who had been in love like that? Was it Caius who could conduct a court session like that?

And Caius is indeed mortal, and it's right that he die, but for me, Vanya, Ivan Ilyich, with all my feelings and thoughts—for me it's another matter. And it cannot be that I should die. It would be too terrible.

So it felt to him.

"If I was to die like Caius, I would have known it, my inner voice would have told me so, but there was nothing of the sort in me; and I and all my friends understood that things were quite otherwise than with Caius. And now look!" he said to himself. "It can't be. It can't be, but it is. How can it be? How can I understand it?"

And he could not understand and tried to drive this thought away as false, incorrect, morbid, and to dislodge it with other correct, healthy thoughts. But this thought, not only a thought but as if a reality, came back again and stood before him.

And he called up a series of other thoughts in place of this thought, in hopes of finding support in them. He tried to go back to his former ways of thinking, which had screened him formerly from the thought of death. But—strange thing—all that had formerly screened, hidden, wiped out the consciousness of death now could no longer produce that effect. Lately Ivan Ilyich had spent most of his time in these attempts to restore the former ways of feeling that had screened him from death. He would say to himself: "I'll busy myself with work—why, I used to live by it." And he would go to court, driving away all doubts; he would get into conversation with colleagues and sit down, by old habit absentmindedly, pensively glancing around at the crowd and placing his two emaciated arms on the armrests of the oaken chair, leaning over as usual to a colleague, drawing a brief towards him, exchanging whispers, and then, suddenly raising his eyes and sitting up straight, would pronounce certain words and begin the proceedings. But suddenly in the midst of it the pain in his side, paying no attention to the stage the proceedings had reached, would begin *its own* gnawing work. Ivan Ilyich sensed it, drove the thought of it away, but it would go on, and *it* would come and stand directly in front of him and look at him, and he would be dumbstruck, the light would go out in his eyes, and he would again begin asking himself: "Can *it* alone be true?" And his colleagues and subordinates would be surprised and upset to see that he, such a brilliant and subtle judge, was confused, was making mistakes. He would rouse himself, try to come to his senses, and somehow bring the session to an end and return home with the sad awareness that his work in court could no longer, as before, conceal from him what he wanted concealed; that by his work in court he could not rid himself of *it*. And what was worst of all was that *it* drew him to itself not so that he would do something, but only so that he should look it straight in the eye, look at it and, doing nothing, suffer inexpressibly.

And to save himself from this state, Ivan Ilyich looked for consolation, for other screens, and other screens appeared and for a short time seemed to save him, but at once they were again not so much destroyed as made transparent, as if *it* penetrated everything and there was no screening it out.

It happened in this latter time that he would go into the drawing room he had decorated—into that drawing room where he had fallen, for which—as he laughed venomously to think—for the arranging of which he had sacrificed his life, because he knew that his illness had begun with that bruise—he would go in and see that something had made a scratch on the varnished table. He would look for the cause and find it in the bronze ornamentation of an album, the edge of which was bent. He would pick up the album, an expensive thing he had put together with love, and become vexed at his daughter's and her friends' carelessness— here a torn page, there some photographs turned upside down. He would diligently put it all in order and bend back the ornamentation.

Then it would occur to him to transfer this whole *établissement** with the albums to another corner, near the flowers. He would call a servant: his daughter or his wife would come to help him; they would disagree, contradict him, he would argue, get angry; but all was well, because he did not remember about *it, it* was not seen.

But then his wife would say, as he was moving the objects himself: "Let the servants do it, you'll do harm to yourself again," and suddenly *it* would flash from behind the screen, he would see *it*. *It* flashes, he still hopes *it* will disappear, but he involuntarily senses his side—there sits the same thing, gnawing in the same way, and he can no longer forget it, and *it* clearly stares at him from behind the flowers. What is it all for?

"And it's true that I lost my life here, over this curtain, as if I was storming a fortress. Can it be? How terrible and how stupid! It can't be! Can't be, but is."

He would go to his study, lie down, and again remain alone with *it*. Face to face with *it*, and there was nothing to be done with *it*. Only look at *it* and go cold.

* Establishment.

VII

HOW IT CAME about in the third month of Ivan Ilyich's illness it was impossible to say, because it came about step by step, imperceptibly, but what came about was that his wife, and daughter, and son, and the servants, and acquaintances, and the doctors, and, above all, he himself— knew that for others the whole interest in him consisted only in how soon he would finally vacate his place, free the living from the constraint caused by his presence, and be freed himself from his sufferings.

He slept less and less; they gave him opium and began injections of morphine. But that did not relieve him. The dull anguish he experienced in a half-sleeping state only relieved him at first as something new, but then became as much or still more of a torment than outright pain.

Special foods were prepared for him by the doctors' prescription; but these foods became more and more tasteless, more and more disgusting to him.

Special arrangements were also made for his stools, and this was a torment to him each time. A torment in its uncleanness, indecency, and smell, in the awareness that another person had to take part in it.

But in this most unpleasant matter there also appeared a consolation for Ivan Ilyich. The butler's helper, Gerasim, always came to clear away after him.

Gerasim was a clean, fresh young muzhik, grown sleek on town grub. Always cheerful, bright. At first the sight of this man, always clean, dressed Russian style, performing this repulsive chore, embarrassed Ivan Ilyich.

Once, having gotten up from the commode and being unable to pull up his trousers, he collapsed into the soft armchair, looking with horror at his naked, strengthless thighs with their sharply outlined muscles.

Gerasim, in heavy boots, spreading around him the pleasant smell of boot tar and the freshness of winter air, came in with a light, strong step, in a clean canvas apron and a clean cotton shirt, the sleeves rolled up on his bared, strong, young arms, and without looking at Ivan Ilyich— obviously restraining the joy of life shining on his face, so as not to offend the sick man—went to the commode.

"Gerasim," Ivan Ilyich said weakly.

Gerasim gave a start, evidently afraid he was remiss in something, and with a quick movement he turned to the sick man his fresh, kind, simple young face, only just beginning to sprout a beard.

"What, sir?"

"I suppose this must be unpleasant for you. Excuse me. I can't help it."

"Mercy, sir." And Gerasim flashed his eyes and bared his young, white teeth. "Why shouldn't I do it? It's a matter of you being sick."

And with his deft, strong hands he did his usual business and went out, stepping lightly. And five minutes later, stepping just as lightly, he came back.

Ivan Ilyich was still sitting the same way in the armchair.

"Gerasim," he said, when the man had set down the clean, washed commode, "help me, please. Come here." Gerasim went to him. "Lift me up. It's hard for me alone, and I've sent Dmitri away."

Gerasim went to him. With his strong arms, just as lightly as he stepped, he embraced him, deftly and softly lifted and held him, pulling his trousers up with the other hand, and was about to sit him down. But Ivan Ilyich asked him to lead him to the sofa. Gerasim, effortlessly and as if without pressure, led him, almost carried him, to the sofa and sat him down.

"Thank you. How deftly, how well . . . you do it all."

Gerasim smiled again and was about to leave. But Ivan Ilyich felt so good with him that he did not want to let him go.

"I tell you what: move that chair for me, please. No, that one, under my legs. It's a relief for me when my legs are raised."

Gerasim brought the chair, set it down noiselessly, lowering it all at once right to the floor, and placed Ivan Ilyich's legs on it; it seemed to Ivan Ilyich that it was a relief for him when Gerasim lifted his legs high.

"I feel better when my legs are raised," said Ivan Ilyich. "Put that pillow under for me."

Gerasim did so. Again he lifted his legs and set them down. Again Ivan Ilyich felt better while Gerasim was holding his legs. When he lowered them, it seemed worse.

"Gerasim," he said to him, "are you busy now?"

"By no means, sir," said Gerasim, who had learned from the townspeople how to talk with gentlefolk.

"What more have you got to do?"

"What's there for me to do? I've done everything except split the wood for tomorrow."

"Then hold my legs a little higher, can you?"

"That I can." Gerasim lifted his legs higher, and it seemed to Ivan Ilych that in that position he felt no pain at all.

"But what about the wood?"

"Please don't worry, sir. There'll be time."

Ivan Ilyich told Gerasim to sit and hold his legs, and he conversed with him. And—strange thing—it seemed to him that he felt better while Gerasim held his legs.

After that Ivan Ilyich occasionally summoned Gerasim and made him hold his legs on his shoulders, and he liked talking with him. Gerasim did it easily, willingly, simply, and with a kindness that moved Ivan Ilyich. Health, strength, vigor of life in all other people offended Ivan Ilyich; only Gerasim's strength and vigor of life did not distress but soothed him.

The main torment for Ivan Ilyich was the lie, that lie for some reason acknowledged by everyone, that he was merely ill and not dying, and that he needed only to keep calm and be treated, and then something very good would come of it. While he knew that whatever they did, nothing would come of it except still more tormenting suffering and death. And he was tormented by that lie, tormented that no one wanted to acknowledge what they all knew and he knew, but wanted to lie to him about his terrible situation, and wanted him and even forced him to participate in that lie. The lie, this lie, perpetrated upon him on the eve of his death, the lie that must needs reduce the dreadful, solemn act of his death to the level of all their visits, curtains, sturgeon dinners . . . was terribly tormenting for Ivan Ilyich. And—strangely—many times, as they were performing their tricks over him, he was a hair's breadth from shouting at them: "Stop lying! You know and I know that I'm dying, so at least stop lying." But he never had the courage to do it. The dreadful, terrible act of his dying, he saw, was reduced by all those around him to the level of an accidental unpleasantness, partly an indecency (something like dealing with a man who comes into a drawing room spreading a bad smell), in the name of that very "decency" he had served all his life; he saw that no one would feel sorry for him, because no one even wanted to understand his situation. Only Gerasim understood that situation and pitied him. And therefore Ivan Ilyich felt good only with Gerasim. It felt good to him when Gerasim held his legs up, sometimes all night long, and refused to go to sleep, saying: "Please don't worry, Ivan Ilyich, I'll still get some sleep"; or when, suddenly addressing him familiarly, he added: "Maybe if you weren't sick, but why not be a help?" Gerasim alone did not lie, everything showed that he alone understood what it was all about, and did not find it necessary to conceal it, and simply pitied his emaciated, weakened master. Once he even said straight out, as Ivan Ilyich was sending him away: "We'll all die. Why not take the trouble?"—expressing by that that he was not burdened by his trouble precisely because he was bearing it for a dying man and hoped that when his time came someone would go to the same trouble for him.

Apart from this lie, or owing to it, the most tormenting thing for Ivan Ilyich was that no one pitied him as he wanted to be pitied: there were moments, after prolonged suffering, when Ivan Ilyich wanted most of all, however embarrassed he would have been to admit it, to be pitied by someone like a sick child. He wanted to be caressed, kissed, wept over, as children are caressed and comforted. He knew that he was an important judge, that he had a graying beard, and that therefore it was impossible; but he wanted it all the same. And in his relations with Gerasim there was something close to it, and therefore his relations with Gerasim comforted him. Ivan Ilyich wanted to weep, wanted to be caressed and wept over, and then comes his colleague, the judge Shebek, and instead of weeping and caressing, Ivan Ilyich makes a serious, stern, profoundly thoughtful face and, by inertia, gives his opinion on the significance of a decision of the appeals court and stubbornly insists on it. This lie around and within him poisoned most of all the last days of Ivan Ilyich's life.

VIII

IT WAS MORNING. It was morning if only because Gerasim had gone and the servant Pyotr had come, put out the candles, drawn one curtain, and quietly begun tidying up. Whether it was morning or evening, Friday or Sunday, was all the same, all one and the same: a gnawing, tormenting pain, never subsiding for a moment; the awareness of life ever hopelessly going but never quite gone; always the same dreadful, hateful death approaching—the sole reality now—and always the same lie. What were days, weeks, and hours here?

"Would you care for tea, sir?"

"He needs order, so his masters should have tea in the mornings," he thought, and said only:

"No."

"Would you like to lie on the sofa?"

"He needs to tidy up the room, and I'm in his way, I am uncleanness, disorder," he thought, and said only:

"No, let me be."

The servant pottered around some more. Ivan Ilyich reached out his hand. Pyotr obligingly came over.

"What can I do for you, sir?"

"My watch."

Pyotr picked up the watch, which was lying just by his hand, and gave it to him.

"Half past eight. Are they up yet?"

"No, sir. Vassily Ivanovich" (that was the son) "has gone to school, and Praskovya Fyodorovna gave orders to wake her if you asked for her. Shall I do so?"

"No, don't." "Shouldn't I try some tea?" he thought. "Yes . . . bring tea."

Pyotr went to the door. Ivan Ilyich was afraid to be left alone. "How can I keep him? Ah, yes, my medicine." "Pyotr, give me my medicine." "Who knows, maybe the medicine will still help." He took a spoonful and swallowed it. "No, it won't help. It's all nonsense, deception," he decided as soon as he tasted the familiar sickly sweet and hopeless taste. "No, I can't believe it any more. But the pain, why the pain? If only it would stop for a moment." And he moaned. Pyotr turned back. "No, go. Bring the tea."

Pyotr went out. Ivan Ilyich, left alone, moaned not so much from pain, terrible though it was, as from anguish. "Always the same, always the same, all these endless days and nights. Let it be sooner. What sooner? Death, darkness. No, no. Anything's better than death!"

When Pyotr came in with the tea tray, Ivan Ilyich looked at him for a long time in perplexity, not understanding who and what he was. Pyotr became embarrassed under this gaze. And when Pyotr became embarrassed, Ivan Ilyich came to his senses.

"Ah, yes," he said, "the tea . . . good, set it down. Only help me to wash and put on a clean shirt."

And Ivan Ilyich began to wash. With pauses for rest, he washed his hands, his face, brushed his teeth, started combing his hair, and looked in the mirror. He became frightened; especially frightening was how his hair lay flat on his pale forehead.

While his shirt was being changed, he knew he would be still more frightened if he looked at his body, so he did not look at himself. But now it was all over. He put on his dressing gown, wrapped himself in a plaid, and sat down in the armchair to have tea. For a moment he felt refreshed, but as soon as he began to drink the tea, there was again the same taste, the same pain. He forced himself to finish it and lay down, stretching his legs. He lay down and dismissed Pyotr.

Always the same thing. A drop of hope glimmers, then a sea of despair begins to rage, and always the pain, always the pain, always the anguish, always one and the same thing. Being alone is a horrible anguish, he wants to call someone, but he knows beforehand that with others it is still worse. "At least morphine again—to become oblivious. I'll tell him, the doctor, to think up something else. It's impossible like this, impossible."

An hour, two hours pass in this way. But now there's a ringing in the front hall. Could be the doctor. Right, it's the doctor, fresh, brisk, fat, cheerful, with an expression that says: So you're scared of something here, but we'll fix it all up for you in no time. The doctor knows that this expression is unsuitable here, but he has put it on once and for all and cannot take it off, like a man who puts on a tailcoat in the morning and goes around visiting.

The doctor rubs his hands briskly, comfortingly.

"I'm cold. It's freezing outside. Let me warm up," he says with such an expression as if they only had to wait a little till he warmed up, and when he warmed up, he would put everything right.

"Well, how . . . ?"

Ivan Ilyich senses that the doctor would like to say "How's every little thing?" but that he, too, senses that he cannot say that, and so he says: "How was your night?"

Ivan Ilyich looks at the doctor with a questioning expression: "Will you never be ashamed of lying?" But the doctor does not want to understand the question.

And Ivan Ilyich says:

"Terrible as ever. The pain doesn't go away, doesn't let up. If you could do something!"

"Ah, you sick people are always like that. Well, sir, now I seem to be warm; even the most exacting Praskovya Fyodorovna could make no objection to my temperature. Well, sir, greetings." And the doctor shakes his hand.

And, setting aside all his earlier playfulness, the doctor begins with a serious air to examine the sick man, takes his pulse, his temperature, and then gets to the tappings, the auscultations.

Ivan Ilyich knows firmly and indubitably that this is all nonsense and empty deception, but when the doctor, getting on his knees, stretches out, putting his ear now higher, now lower, and with a most significant face performs various gymnastic evolutions over him, Ivan Ilyich succumbs to it, as he used to succumb to lawyers' speeches, when he knew very well they were all lies and why they were lies.

The doctor, kneeling on the sofa, was still doing his tapping when the silk dress of Praskovya Fyodorovna rustled in the doorway and she was heard reproaching Pyotr for not announcing the doctor's arrival to her.

She comes in, kisses her husband, and at once begins to insist that she was up long ago and it was only by misunderstanding that she was not there when the doctor came.

Ivan Ilyich looks at her, examines her all over, and reproaches her for her whiteness, and plumpness, and the cleanness of her hands, her neck, the glossiness of her hair, and the sparkle of her eyes, so full of life. He hates her with all the forces of his soul. And her touch makes him suffer from a flood of hatred for her.

Her attitude towards him and his illness is ever the same. As the doctor had developed in himself an attitude towards his patients which he was unable to take off, so she had developed a certain attitude towards him—that he had not done something he should have, and he himself was to blame, and she lovingly reproached him for it—and she could no longer take off this attitude towards him.

"He simply doesn't listen! Doesn't take his medicine on time. And above all, he lies in a position which is surely bad for him—legs up."

She told about how he made Gerasim hold his legs.

The doctor smiled with kindly disdain, meaning: "No help for it, these sick people sometimes think up such foolishness; but it's forgivable."

When the examination was over, the doctor looked at his watch, and then Praskovya Fyodorovna announced to Ivan Ilyich that, whether he liked it or not, she had invited a famous doctor that day, and he would examine him and consult with Mikhail Danilovich (as the usual doctor was called).

"Don't resist, please. I'm doing it for myself," she said ironically, letting it be felt that she was doing it all for him, and that alone gave him no right to refuse. He said nothing and scowled. He felt that this lie surrounding him was so entangled that it was hard to sort anything out.

Everything she did for him she did only for herself, and she said to him that she was doing for herself that which she was in fact doing for herself, as if it was such an incredible thing that he would have to understand it inversely.

Indeed, at half past eleven the famous doctor arrived. Again there were auscultations and significant conversations in his presence and in the next room about the kidney, about the appendix, and questions and answers with such a significant air that again, instead of the real question of life and death, which now alone confronted him, there re-emerged the question of the kidney and the appendix, which were not behaving as they should, and for which Mikhail Danilovich and the famous doctor were about to fall upon them and make them mend their ways.

The famous doctor took his leave with a serious but not hopeless air. And to the timid question which Ivan Ilyich addressed to him, raising his eyes glittering with fear and hope, whether there was a possibility of recovery, he replied that, though he could not vouch for it, there was such a possibility. The hopeful look with which Ivan Ilyich saw the doctor off was so pitiful that, on seeing it, Praskovya Fyodorovna even burst into tears as she came out of the study to hand the famous doctor his honorarium.

The boost in his spirits produced by the doctor's reassurance did not last long. Again the same room, the same paintings, curtains, wallpaper, vials, and his same sick, suffering body. And Ivan Ilyich began to moan; he was given an injection and became oblivious.

When he came to, it was getting dark; his dinner was brought. He forced himself to swallow some bouillon; and again the same thing, and again the approach of night.

After dinner, at seven o'clock, Praskovya Fyodorovna came into his room dressed for the evening, with fat, tight-laced breasts, and with traces of powder on her face. She had already reminded him in the morning that they were going to the theater. Sarah Bernhardt[10] was visiting, and they had a box he had insisted on taking. Now he had forgotten about it, and her outfit offended him. But he concealed his offense when he remembered that he himself had insisted that they get a box and go, because it was an educational aesthetic pleasure for the children.

Praskovya Fyodorovna came in pleased with herself, but as if guilty. She sat down, asked about his health, as he could see, only in order to ask, not in order to find out, knowing that there was nothing to find out, and began telling him what she had in mind: that they would not have gone for anything, but the box had been taken, that Hélène and their daughter and Petrishchev (the examining magistrate, the daughter's fiancé) were going, and that it was impossible to let them go alone. And that otherwise she would have liked better to sit with him. Only he should do what the doctor had prescribed in her absence.

"Ah, yes, and Fyodor Petrovich" (the fiancé) "wanted to come in. Can he? And Liza."

"Let them."

The daughter came in all dressed up, with her young body bared, that body which made him suffer so. Yet she exposed it. Strong, healthy, obviously in love, and indignant at the illness, suffering, and death that interfered with her happiness.

Fyodor Petrovich came in, too, in a tailcoat, his hair curled *à la Capoule*,[11] with a long, sinewy neck closely encased in a white collar, with an enormous white shirt front and narrow black trousers tightly stretched over his strong thighs, with a white glove drawn onto one hand, and holding an opera hat.

After him a little schoolboy crept in inconspicuously, in a new uniform, the poor lad, wearing gloves, and with terrible blue circles under his eyes, the meaning of which Ivan Ilyich knew.

He had always pitied his son. And his frightened and commiserating glance was dreadful for him. Apart from Gerasim, it seemed to Ivan Ilyich that Vasya alone understood and pitied him.

They all sat down and asked again about his health. Silence ensued. Liza asked her mother about the opera glasses. An altercation ensued between mother and daughter about who had done what with them. It was unpleasant.

Fyodor Petrovich asked Ivan Ilyich whether he had seen Sarah Bernhardt. At first Ivan Ilyich did not understand what he was being asked, and then he said:

"No, have you?"

"Yes, in *Adrienne Lecouvreur.*"[12]

Praskovya Fyodorovna said she had been especially good in something or other. The daughter objected. A conversation began about the gracefulness and realism of her acting—that very conversation which is always one and the same.

In the middle of the conversation, Fyodor Petrovich glanced at Ivan Ilyich and fell silent. The others glanced at him and fell silent. Ivan Ilyich was staring straight ahead with glittering eyes, obviously indignant with them. This had to be rectified, but it was quite impossible to rectify it. This silence had to be broken somehow. No one ventured to do it, and they all became frightened that the decorous lie would somehow be violated, and what was there would be clear to all. Liza was the first to venture. She broke the silence. She wanted to conceal what they all felt, but she let it slip.

"Anyhow, *if we're going*, it's time," she said, glancing at her watch, a gift from her father, and smiling barely perceptibly to the young man about something known only to them, and she stood up, her dress rustling.

They all stood up, said good-bye, and left.

When they were gone, it seemed a relief to Ivan Ilyich: there was no lie—it had gone with them—but the pain remained. The same pain, the same fear made it so that nothing was harder, nothing was easier. It was all worse.

Again minute followed minute, hour hour, always the same, and always without end, and always more frightening the inevitable end.

"Yes, send Gerasim," he replied to Pyotr's question.

IX

LATE THAT NIGHT his wife returned. She came in on tiptoe, but he heard her: he opened his eyes and hastily closed them. She wanted to send Gerasim away and sit with him herself. He opened his eyes and said:

"No. Go away."

"Are you suffering very much?"

"It makes no difference."

"Take some opium."

He agreed and drank it. She left.

Until about three he lay in tormenting oblivion. It seemed to him that they were pushing him painfully into some narrow and deep black sack, and kept pushing him further, and could not push him through. And this thing, which is terrible for him, is being accomplished with suffering. And he is afraid, and yet he wants to fall through, and he struggles, and he helps. And then suddenly he lost hold and fell, and came to his senses. The same Gerasim is sitting at the foot of the bed, dozing calmly, patiently. And he is lying with his emaciated legs in stockings placed on Gerasim's shoulders; the same candle with its shade, and the same unceasing pain.

"Go away, Gerasim," he whispered.

"Never mind, I'll stay, sir."

"No, go away."

He took his legs down, lay sideways on his arm, and felt sorry for himself. He waited only until Gerasim went to the next room, and then stopped holding himself back and wept like a child. He wept over his helplessness, over his terrible loneliness, over the cruelty of people, over the cruelty of God, over the absence of God.

"Why have You done all this? Why have You brought me here? Why, why do You torment me so terribly? . . ."

He did not expect an answer and wept that there was not and could not be an answer. The pain rose up again, but he did not stir, did not call out. He kept saying to himself: "Well, go on, beat me! But what for? What have I done to You? What for?"

Then he quieted down, not only stopped weeping, but stopped breathing, and became all attention: it was as if he were listening not to a voice that spoke in sounds, but to the voice of his soul, to the course of thoughts arising in him.

"What do you want?" was the first clear idea, expressible in words, that he heard. "What do you want? What do you want?" he repeated to himself. "What? Not to suffer. To live," he replied.

And again he gave himself entirely to such intense attention that even the pain did not distract him.

"To live? To live how?" asked the voice of his soul.

"Yes, to live as I lived before: nicely, pleasantly."

"As you lived before, nicely and pleasantly?" asked the voice. And he started to go over in his imagination the best moments of his pleasant life. But—strange thing—all those best moments of his pleasant life seemed now not at all as they had seemed then. All—except for his first memories of childhood. There, in childhood, there had been something really pleasant, which one could live with if it came back. But the man who had experienced that pleasure was no more: it was as if the memory was about someone else.

As soon as that began the result of which was he, the Ivan Ilyich of today, all that had then seemed like joys melted away and turned into something worthless and often vile.

And the further from childhood, the closer to the present, the more worthless and dubious were those joys. It began with law school. There had still been some truly good things there: there had been merriment, there had been friendship, there had been hopes. But in the higher grades those good moments had already become more rare. Then, during the initial time of working for the governor, there had again been good moments: these were his memories of love for a woman. Then it all became confused, and there was still less that was good. And further on still less of the good, and the further, the less.

His marriage . . . so accidental, and the disenchantment, and the smell of his wife's breath, and the sensuality, the dissembling! And this deadly service, and these worries about money, and that for a year, and two, and ten, and twenty—and all of it the same. And the further, the deadlier. As if I was going steadily downhill, while imagining I was going up. And so it was. In public opinion I was going uphill, and exactly to that extent life was slipping away from under me . . . And now that's it, so die!

But what is this? Why? It can't be. Can it be that life is so meaningless and vile? And if it is indeed so vile and meaningless, then why die, and die suffering? Something's not right.

"Maybe I did not live as I should have?" would suddenly come into his head. "But how not, if I did everything one ought to?" he would say to himself and at once drive this sole solution to the whole riddle of life and death away from him as something completely impossible.

"What do you want now, then? To live? To live how? To live as you live in court, when the usher proclaims: 'Court is in session!' Court is in session, court is in session," he repeated to himself. "Here is that court! But I'm not guilty!" he cried out angrily. "What for?" And he stopped weeping and, turning his face to the wall, began to think about one and the same thing: why, what for, all this horror?

But however much he thought, he found no answer. And when it occurred to him, as it often did, that it was all happening because he had not lived right, he at once recalled all the correctness of his life and drove this strange thought away.

X

ANOTHER TWO WEEKS went by. Ivan Ilyich no longer got up from the sofa. He did not want to lie in bed and so he lay on the sofa. And, lying almost always face to the wall, he suffered all alone the same insoluble suffering and thought all alone the same insoluble thought. What is this? Can it be true that it is death? And an inner voice replied: Yes, it's true. Why these torments? And the voice replied: Just so, for no reason. Beyond and besides that there was nothing.

From the very beginning of his illness, from the time when Ivan Ilyich first went to the doctor, his life had divided into two opposite states of mind, which alternated with each other: now there was despair and the expectation of an incomprehensible and terrible death, now there was hope and the interest-filled process of observing the functioning of his body. Now there hung before his eyes a kidney or an intestine that shirked its duty for a time; now there was only incomprehensible, terrible death, from which there was no escape.

These two states of mind had alternated from the very beginning of the illness; but the further the illness went, the more dubious and fantastic became the considerations of the kidney and the more real the awareness of approaching death.

He needed only to recall what he had been three months ago and what he was now, to recall how steadily he had gone downhill, for any possibility of hope to be destroyed.

In the recent time of that solitude in which he found himself, lying face to the back of the sofa, that solitude in the midst of the populous town and his numerous acquaintances and family—a solitude than which there could be none more total anywhere: not at the bottom of the sea, not under the earth—in the recent time of that dreadful solitude, Ivan Ilyich had lived only on imaginings of the past. One after another, pictures of the past appeared to him. They always began with the nearest time and went back to the most remote, to childhood, and there they stayed. If Ivan Ilyich recalled the stewed prunes he had been given to eat that day, he then recalled the raw, shriveled French prunes of his childhood, their special taste, the abundant saliva when it got as far as the stone, and alongside this memory of taste emerged a whole series of memories from that time: his nanny, his brother, his toys. "Mustn't think about that . . . too painful," Ivan Ilyich said to himself and shifted back to the present. A button on the back of the sofa and the puckered morocco. "Morocco's expensive, flimsy; there was a quarrel over it. But there was another morocco and another quarrel, when we tore our father's briefcase and were punished, and mama brought us little pies." And again it stayed with childhood, and again it was painful for Ivan Ilyich, and he tried to drive it away and think of something else.

And again right there, along with this course of recollection, another course of recollection was going on in his soul—of how his illness had grown and worsened. The further back it went, the more life there was. There was more goodness in life, and more of life itself. The two merged together. "As my torment kept getting worse and worse, so the whole of life got worse and worse," he thought. There was one bright spot back there, at the beginning of life, and then it became ever darker and darker, ever quicker and quicker. "In inverse proportion to the square of the distance from death," thought Ivan Ilyich. And this image of a stone plunging down with increasing speed sank into his soul. Life, a series of ever-increasing sufferings, races faster and faster towards its end, the most dreadful suffering. "I'm racing . . ." He would give a start, rouse himself, want to resist; but he already knew that it was impossible to resist, and again, with eyes weary from looking, but unable not to look at what was before him, he gazed at the back of the sofa and waited—waited for that dreadful fall, impact, and destruction. "It's impossible to resist," he said to himself. "But at least to understand what for? Even that is impossible. It would be possible to explain it, if I were to say to myself that I have not lived as one ought. But that cannot possibly be acknowledged," he said to himself, recalling all the legitimacy, regularity, and decency of his life. "To admit that is quite impossible," he said to himself, his lips smiling, as if there were someone to see that smile and be deceived by it. "There's no explanation! Torment, death . . . What for?"

XI

So TWO WEEKS WENT BY. During those weeks an event desired by Ivan Ilyich and his wife took place: Petrishchev made a formal proposal. This took place in the evening. The next day Praskovya Fyodorovna came to her husband's room, pondering how to announce Fyodor Petrovich's proposal to him, but the previous night a new change for the worse had occurred in Ivan Ilyich. Praskovya Fyodorovna found him on the same sofa, but in a new position. He was lying on his back, moaning, and staring straight in front of him with a fixed gaze.

She started talking about medicines. He shifted his gaze to her. She did not finish what she had begun: such spite, precisely against her, was expressed in that gaze.

"For Christ's sake, let me die in peace," he said.

She was going to leave, but just then their daughter came in and went over to greet him. He looked at his daughter in the same way as at his wife, and to her questions about his health said drily to her that he would soon free them all of himself. They both fell silent, sat for a while, and left.

"What fault is it of ours?" Liza said to her mother. "As if we did anything! I feel sorry for papa, but why torment us?"

The doctor came at the usual time. Ivan Ilyich answered "Yes" and "No," without taking his spiteful gaze from him, and in the end said:

"You know you can't help at all, so leave off."

"We can ease your suffering," said the doctor.

"Even that you can't do. Leave off."

The doctor came out to the drawing room and informed Praskovya Fyodorovna that things were very bad and that the only remedy was opium to ease his sufferings, which must be terrible.

The doctor said that his physical sufferings were terrible, and that was true; but more terrible than his physical sufferings were his moral sufferings, and these were his chief torment.

His moral sufferings consisted in the fact that, looking at Gerasim's sleepy, good-natured, high-cheekboned face that night, it had suddenly occurred to him: And what if my whole life, my conscious life, has indeed been "not right"?

It occurred to him that what had formerly appeared completely impossible to him, that he had not lived his life as he should have, might be true. It occurred to him that those barely noticeable impulses he had felt to fight against what highly placed people considered good, barely noticeable impulses which he had immediately driven away—that they might have been the real thing, and all the rest might have been not right. His work, and his living conditions, and his family, and these social and professional interests—all might have been not right. He tried to defend it all to himself. And he suddenly felt all the weakness of what he was defending. And there was nothing to defend.

"But if that's so," he said to himself, "and I am quitting this life with the consciousness that I have ruined everything that was given me, and it is impossible to rectify it, what then?" He lay on his back and started going over his whole life in a totally new way. In the morning, when he saw the footman, then his wife, then his daughter, then the doctor—their every movement, their every word confirmed the terrible truth revealed to him that night. In them he saw himself, all that he had lived by, and saw clearly that it was all not right, that it was all a terrible, vast deception concealing both life and death. This consciousness increased his physical sufferings tenfold. He moaned, and thrashed, and tore at his clothes. It seemed to be choking and crushing him. And for that he hated them.

He was given a large dose of opium and became oblivious; but at dinnertime the same thing began again. He drove everyone away and thrashed from side to side.

His wife came to him and said:

"Jean, darling, do this for me" (for me?). "It can't do any harm and often helps. It's really nothing. Even healthy people often . . ."

He opened his eyes wide.

"What? Take communion? Why? There's no need! Although . . ."
She began to cry.

"Yes, my dear? I'll send for ours, he's so nice."

"Excellent, very good," he said.

When the priest came and confessed him, he softened, felt a sort of relief from his doubts and consequently from his sufferings, and a moment of hope came over him. He began thinking about the appendix again and the possibility of its mending. He took communion with tears in his eyes.

When they laid him down after communion, he felt eased for a moment, and hopes of life appeared again. He began to think about the operation that had been suggested to him. "To live, I want to live," he said to himself. His wife came to congratulate him on his communion; she said the usual words and added:

"Isn't it true you're feeling better?"

He said "Yes" without looking at her.

Her clothes, her figure, the expression of her face, the sound of her voice—all told him one thing: "Not right. All that you've lived and live by is a lie, a deception, concealing life and death from you." And as soon as he thought it, his hatred arose and together with hatred his tormenting physical sufferings and with his sufferings the consciousness of near, inevitable destruction. Something new set in: twisting, and shooting, and choking his breath.

The expression of his face when he said "Yes" was terrible. Having uttered this "Yes," he looked her straight in the face, turned over with a quickness unusual in his weak state, and shouted:

"Go away, go away, leave me alone!"

XII

FROM THAT MOMENT began a three-day ceaseless howling, which was so terrible that it was impossible to hear it without horror even through two closed doors. The moment he answered his wife, he realized that he was lost, that there was no return, that the end had come, the final end, and his doubt was still not resolved, it still remained doubt.

"Oh! Ohh! Oh!" he howled in various intonations. He began by howling, "I won't!" and so went on howling on the letter O.

For all three days, in the course of which there was no time for him, he was thrashing about in that black sack into which an invisible, invincible force was pushing him. He struggled as one condemned to death struggles in the executioner's hands, knowing he cannot save himself; and with every moment he felt that, despite all his efforts to struggle, he was coming closer and closer to what terrified him. He felt that his torment lay in being thrust into that black hole, and still more in being unable to get into it. What kept him from getting into it was the claim that his had been a good life. This justification of his life clutched at him, would not let him move forward, and tormented him most of all.

Suddenly some force shoved him in the chest, in the side, choked his breath still more, he fell through the hole, and there, at the end of the hole, something lit up. What was done to him was like what happens on the train, when you think you are moving forward, but are moving backward, and suddenly find out the real direction.

"Yes, it was all not right," he said to himself, "but never mind. I can, I can do 'right.' But what is 'right'?" he asked himself and suddenly grew still.

This was at the end of the third day, an hour before his death. Just then the little schoolboy quietly stole into his father's room and went up to his bed. The dying man went on howling desperately and thrashing his arms about. His hand landed on the boy's head. The boy seized it, pressed it to his lips, and wept.

Just then Ivan Ilyich fell through, saw light, and it was revealed to him that his life had not been what it ought, but that it could still be rectified. He asked himself what was "right," and grew still, listening. Here he felt that someone was kissing his hand. He opened his eyes and looked at his son. He felt sorry for him. His wife came over to him. He looked at her. She was gazing at him with a despairing expression, openmouthed, and with unwiped tears on her nose and cheek. He felt sorry for her.

"Yes, I'm tormenting them," he thought. "They're sorry, but it will be better for them when I die." He wanted to say that, but was unable to bring it out. "Anyhow, why speak, I must act," he thought. He indicated his son to his wife with his eyes and said:

"Take him away . . . sorry . . . for you, too . . ." He also wanted to say "Forgive," but said "Forgo," and, no longer able to correct himself, waved his hand, knowing that the one who had to would understand.

And suddenly it became clear to him that what was tormenting him and would not be resolved was suddenly all resolved at once, on two sides, on ten sides, on all sides. He was sorry for them, he had to act so that it was not painful for them. To deliver them and deliver himself from these sufferings. "How good and how simple," he thought. "And the pain?" he asked himself. "What's become of it? Where are you, pain?"

He became attentive.

"Yes, there it is. Well, then, let there be pain.

"And death? Where is it?"

He sought his old habitual fear of death and could not find it. Where was it? What death? There was no more fear because there was no more death.

Instead of death there was light.

"So that's it!" he suddenly said aloud. "What joy!"

For him all this happened in an instant and the significance of that instant never changed. For those present, his agony went on for two more hours. Something gurgled in his chest; his emaciated body kept twitching. Then the gurgling and wheezing gradually subsided.

"It's finished!" someone said over him.

He heard those words and repeated them in his soul. "Death is finished," he said to himself. "It is no more."

He drew in air, stopped at mid-breath, stretched out, and died.

1884–86

NOTES

1. *Vint* is a Russian card game similar to auction bridge.

2. In 1722, the emperor Peter the Great (1672–1725) established a table of fourteen ranks for Russian civil servants, rising in importance from fourteenth to first.

3. I. G. Charmeur was a well-known Petersburg tailor of the time.

4. Donon's restaurant, opened by the entrepreneur Zh. B. Donon in 1849, was one of the most fashionable in Petersburg.

5. The Old Believers, also known as Raskolniki (schismatics), rejected the reforms introduced in the mid–seventeenth century by the patriarch Nikon (1605–81), head of the Russian Orthodox Church. Historically, their relations with the civil administration were often strained.

6. The emperor Alexander II (1818–81) carried out a series of important legal reforms in 1864, establishing a new court system and trial by jury, among other things.

7. See note 2 above.

8. The empress Maria Alexandrovna (1824–80), wife of Alexander II, took over the administration of a number of charitable and philanthropic institutions, including the Petersburg Foundling Home, women's educational institutions, and three banks.

9. Johann Gottfried Kiesewetter (1766–1819), German philosopher and follower of Immanuel Kant, was the author of many works, including a manual of logic which was translated into Russian. The syllogism about Caius actually appears in his manual.

10. Sarah Bernhardt (1844–1923), the most famous French actress of her day, performed several times in Russia during the 1880s.

11. That is, combed forward in bangs.

12. A play about the eighteenth-century French actress Adrienne Lecouvreur, by Augustin Scribe (1791–1861) and Gabriel Legouvé (1764–1812). It was one of Sarah Bernhardt's principal roles.